## *The Chronicles of Prydain*
by Lloyd Alexander:

*The Book of Three*

Taran the Assistant Pig-Keeper assembles a group of companions to rescue the oracular pig Hen Wen from the forces of evil.

*The Black Cauldron*

Newbery Honor Book

The warriors of Prydain set out to find and destroy the Black Cauldron, the Death-Lord Arawn's chief instrument of evil.

*The Castle of Llyr*

Princess Eilonwy is growing up and must learn to act like a lady rather than a heroine among heroes.

*Taran Wanderer*

Taran faces a long and lonely search for his identity among the hills and marshes, farmers and common people of Prydain.

*The High King*

Newbery Medal Winner

The final struggle between good and evil dramatically concludes the fate of Prydain, and of Taran who wanted to be a hero.

*Also available:*

*The Foundling and Other Tales of Prydain*

by Lloyd Alexander

Eight short stories evoke the land of Prydain before the adventures of Taran the Assistant Pig-Keeper.

*The Prydain Companion*

*A Reference Guide to Lloyd Alexander's Prydain Chronicles*

by Michael O. Tunnell

# The Foundling

*and Other Tales of Prydain*

# THE FOUNDLING

## *and Other Tales of Prydain*

LLOYD ALEXANDER

HENRY HOLT AND COMPANY
NEW YORK

An Imprint of Macmillan



Library of Congress Cataloging-in-Publication Data
Alexander, Lloyd.
The foundling and other tales of Prydain / by Lloyd Alexander.
p. cm.
ISBN 978-0-8050-8053-7
Summary: Eight short stories dealing with events that preceded the birth of Taran the Assistant Pig-Keeper and key figure in the author's five works on the kingdom of Prydain.
1. Children's stories, American. 2. Fantastic fiction. [1. Fantasy. 2. Short stories.] I. Title.
PZ7.A3774Fno 1999 [Fic]—dc21 98-42807

Originally published in the United States by Henry Holt and Company
First Square Fish Edition: June 2012
Square Fish logo designed by Filomena Tuosto
mackids.com

5 7 9 10 8 6 4

AR: 2.8 / LEXILE: NP

*For Friends of Prydain,*
*who promised to read more*
*if I promised to write more*

# CONTENTS

# Author's Note

Many readers of all ages have asked for a new journey to Prydain, and popular demand makes a splendid pretext for a writer to do what he always wanted to do in the first place. However, the tales offered here are meant to be more than a fond return to the imaginary realm that has been part of my life for some years, not retracing steps but venturing deeper into unmapped territory.

Unlike the adventures beginning with *The Book of Three* and ending with *The High King*, these tales deal with happenings before the birth of Taran Assistant Pig-Keeper. Though short in length, they are, I hope, not lacking in substance. While they take up certain threads left unraveled in the longer weaving, each stands by itself and tries to relate matters bearing not only on the history of Prydain but on our own times and concerns as well. Inspired originally by Welsh legend, the tales, for me, have grown to be much more personal than mythological.

Readers visiting Prydain for the first time in these pages may enjoy them without foreknowledge of events to come. Those who already know the chronicles may be pleased to meet some old friends in different circumstances. Dallben first appears here not as an age-worn enchanter but as a baby floating in a wicker basket in the Marshes of Morva. Doli of the Fair Folk is as frustrated and bad tempered as ever. Princess Angharad, mother of Eilonwy, proves herself as clear-sighted and strong-willed as the daughter she is destined to bear. Medwyn, ancient protector of animals, keeps his patience and compassion despite the antics of Kadwyr, the rascal crow. The grim history of the sword Dyrnwyn is finally revealed, along with the terrible fate of King Rhitta in Spiral Castle. Menwy, the harper, is mentioned only briefly in the previous chronicles; but here, when he cries out defiance of the Death-Lord himself, he counts as a hero in his own right, and his affirmation of life reaches far beyond the boundaries of a fanciful kingdom.

It always startles me to realize how many early friends of Prydain are by now grown men and women, and how young the new friends are. But I hope, in any case, calendar years will be no hindrance to enjoyment, and that the reader will find some of the pleasure these tales have given the writer.

Lloyd Alexander

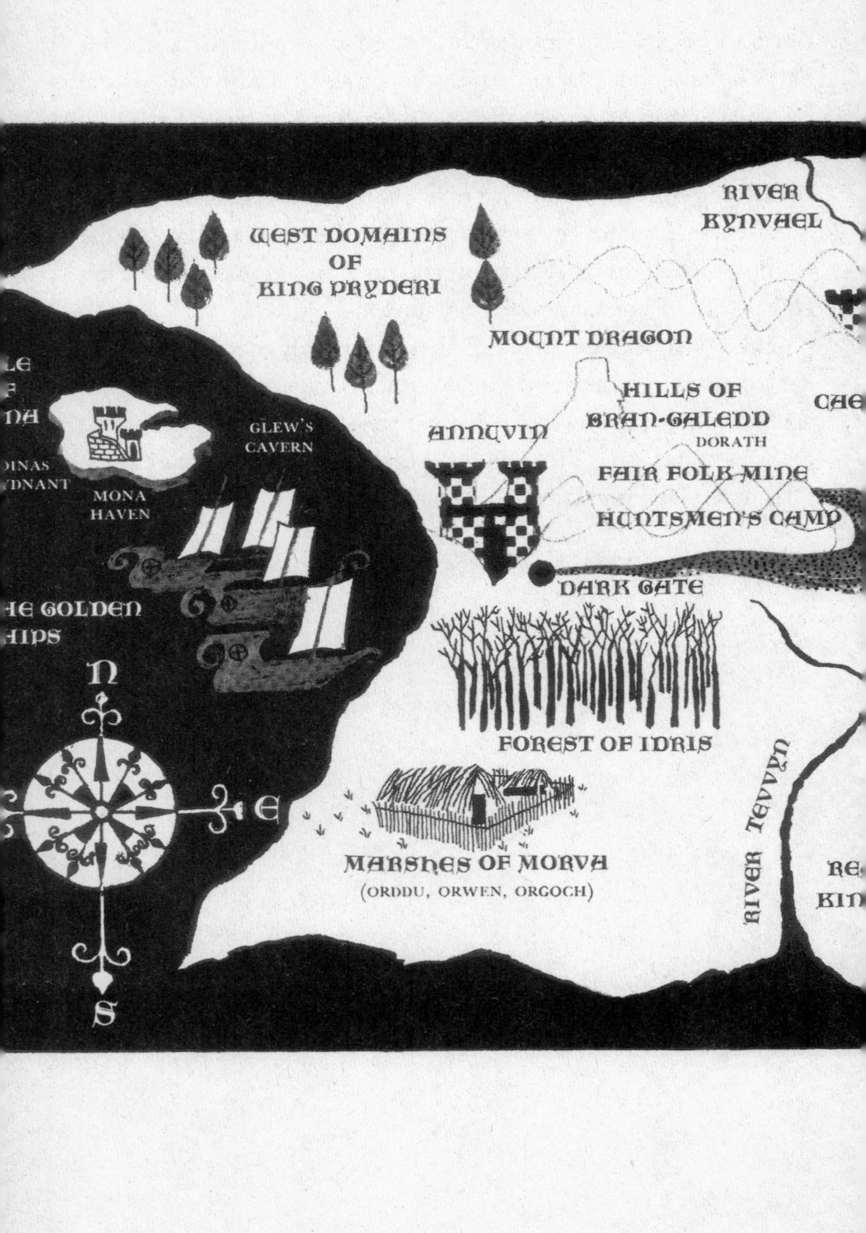
WEST DOMAINS
OF
KING PRYDERI
RIVER
KYNVAEL
MOUNT DRAGON
HILLS OF
BRAN-GALEDD
DORATH
GLEW'S
CAVERN
MONA
HAVEN
ANNUVIN
FAIR FOLK MINE
HUNTSMEN'S CAMP
DARK GATE
N
E
S
FOREST OF IDRIS
RIVER TEVVYN
MARSHES OF MORVA
(ORDDU, ORWEN, ORGOCH)

EASTERN STRONGHOLDS
NORTHERN REALMS
REALM OF THE FAIR FOLK
EAGLE MOUNTAINS
MEDWYN'S VALLEY
THYL
LLAWGADARN MOUNTAINS
RUINED WALL
ISAV
MERIN
E RED FALLOWS
FREE COMMOTS
GWENITH
VALLEY CANTREVS
SMALL AVREN
CENARTH
CAER CADARN
HILL CANTREVS
RIVER YSTRAD
GREAT AVREN
CAER DALLBE

# The Foundling

*and Other Tales of Prydain*

# The Foundling

This is told of Dallben, greatest of enchanters in Prydain: how three black-robed hags found him, when he was still a baby, in a basket at the edge of the Marshes of Morva. "Oh, Orddu, see what's here!" cried the one named Orwen, peering into the wicker vessel floating amid the tall grasses. "Poor lost duckling! He'll catch his death of cold! Whatever shall we do with him?"

"A sweet morsel," croaked the one named Orgoch from the depths of her hood. "A tender lamb. I know what I should do."

"Please be silent, Orgoch," said the one named Orddu. "You've already had your breakfast." Orddu was a short, plump woman with a round, lumpy face and sharp black eyes. Jewels, pins, and brooches glittered in her tangle of weedy hair. "We can't leave him here to get all soggy. I suppose we shall have to take him home with us."

"Oh, yes!" exclaimed Orwen, dangling her string of milky white beads over the tiny figure in the basket. "Ah, the darling tadpole! Look at his pink cheeks and chubby little fingers! He's smiling at us, Orddu! He's waving! But what shall we call him? He mustn't go bare and nameless."

"If you ask me—" began Orgoch.

"No one did," replied Orddu. "You are quite right, Orwen. We must give him a name. Otherwise, how shall we know who he is?"

"We have so many names lying around the cottage," said Orwen. "Some of them never used. Give him a nice, fresh, unwrinkled one."

"There's a charming name I'd been saving for a special occasion," Orddu said, "but I can't remember what I did with it. No matter. His name—his name: Dallben."

"Lovely!" cried Orwen, clapping her hands. "Oh, Orddu, you have such good taste."

"Taste, indeed!" snorted Orgoch. "Dallben? Why call him Dallben?"

"Why not?" returned Orddu. "It will do splendidly. Very good quality, very durable. It should last him a lifetime."

"It will last him," Orgoch muttered, "as long as he needs it."

And so Dallben was named and nursed by these three, and given a home in their cottage near the Marshes of Morva. Under their care he grew sturdy, bright, and fair of face. He was kind and generous, and each day handsomer and happier.

The hags did not keep from him that he was a foundling. But when he was of an age to wonder about such matters, he asked where indeed he had come from, and what the rest of the world was like.

"My dear chicken," replied Orddu, "as to where you came from, we haven't the slightest notion. Nor, might I say, the least interest. You're here with us now, to our delight, and that's quite enough to know."

"As to the rest of the world," Orwen added, "don't bother your pretty, curly head about it. You can be sure it doesn't bother about you. Be glad you were found instead of drowned. Why, this very moment you might be part of a school of fish. And what a slippery, scaly sort of life that would be!"

"I like fish," muttered Orgoch, "especially eels."

"Do hush, dear Orgoch," said Orddu. "You're always thinking of your stomach."

Despite his curiosity, Dallben saw there was no use in questioning further. Cheerful and willing, he went about every task with eagerness and good grace. He drew pails of water from the well, kept the fire burning in the hearth, pumped the bellows, swept away the ashes, and dug the garden. No toil was too troublesome for him. When Orddu spun thread, he turned the spinning wheel. He helped Orwen measure the skeins into lengths and held them for Orgoch to snip with a pair of rusty shears.

One day, when the three brewed a potion of roots and herbs, Dallben was left alone to stir the huge, steaming kettle with a long iron spoon. He obeyed the hags' warning not to taste the liquid, but soon the potion began boiling so briskly that a few drops bubbled up and by accident splashed his fingers. With a cry of pain, Dallben let fall the spoon and popped his fingers into his mouth.

His outcry brought Orddu, Orwen, and Orgoch hurrying back to the cottage.

"Oh, the poor sparrow!" gasped Orwen, seeing the boy sucking at his blistered knuckles. "He's gone and burned himself. I'll fetch an ointment for the sweet fledgling, and some spiderwebs to bandage him. What did you do with all those spiders, Orgoch? They were here only yesterday."

"Too late for all that," growled Orgoch. "Worse damage is done."

"Yes, I'm afraid so," Orddu sighed. "There's no learning without pain. The dear gosling has had his pain; and now, I daresay, he has some learning to go along with it."

Dallben, meanwhile, had swallowed the drops of liquid scalding his fingers. He licked his lips at the taste, sweet and bitter at the same time. And in that instant he began to shake with fear and excitement. All that had been common and familiar in the cottage he saw as he had never seen before.

Now he understood that the leather bellows lying by the hearth commanded the four winds; the pail of water in the corner, the seas and oceans of the world. The earthen floor of the cottage held the roots of all plants and trees. The fire showed him the secrets of its flame, and how all things come to ashes. He gazed awe-struck at the enchantresses, for such they were.

"The threads you spin, and measure, and cut off," Dallben murmured, "these are no threads, but the lives of men. I know who you truly are."

"Oh, I doubt it," Orddu cheerfully answered. "Even we aren't always sure of that. Nevertheless, one taste of that magical brew and you know as much as we do. Almost as much, at any rate."

"Too much for his own good," muttered Orgoch.

"But what shall we do?" moaned Orwen. "He was such a sweet, innocent little robin. If only he hadn't swallowed the potion! Is there no way to make him unswallow it?"

"We could try," said Orgoch.

"No," declared Orddu. "What's done is done. You know that as well as I. Alas, the dear duckling will have to leave us. There's nothing else for it. So many people, knowing so much, under the same roof? All that knowledge crammed in, crowded, bumping and jostling back and forth? We'd not have room to breathe!"

"I say he should be kept," growled Orgoch.

"I don't think he'd like your way of keeping him," Orddu answered. She turned to Dallben. "No, my poor chicken, we must say farewell. You asked us once about the world? I'm afraid you'll have to see it for yourself."

"But, Orddu," protested Orwen, "we can't let him march off just like that. Surely we have some little trinket he'd enjoy? A going-away present, so he won't forget us?"

"I could give him something to remember us by," began Orgoch.

"No doubt," said Orddu. "But that's not what Orwen had in mind. Of course, we shall offer him a gift. Better yet, he shall choose one for himself."

As Dallben watched, the enchantress unlocked an iron-bound chest and rummaged inside, flinging out all sorts of oddments until there was a large heap on the floor.

"Here's something," Orddu at last exclaimed. "Just the thing for a bold young chicken. A sword!"

Dallben caught his breath in wonder as Orddu put the weapon in his hands. The hilt, studded with jewels, glittered so brightly that he was dazzled and nearly blinded. The blade flashed, and a thread of fire ran along its edges.

"Take this, my duckling," Orddu said, "and you shall be the greatest warrior in Prydain. Strength and power, dear gosling! When you command, all must obey even your slightest whim."

"It is a fine blade," Dallben replied, "and comes easily to my hand."

"It shall be yours," Orddu said. "At least, as long as you're able to keep it. Oh, yes," the enchantress went on, "I should mention it's already had a number of owners. Somehow, sooner or later, it wanders back to us. The difficulty, you see, isn't so much getting power as holding on to it. Because so many others want it, too. You'd be astonished, the lengths to which some will go. Be warned, the sword can be lost or stolen. Or bent out of shape—as, indeed, so can you, in a manner of speaking."

"And remember," put in Orwen, "you must never let it out of your sight, not for an instant."

Dallben hesitated a moment, then shook his head. "I think your gift is more burden than blessing."

"In that case," Orddu said, "perhaps this will suit you better."

As Dallben laid down the sword, the enchantress handed him a golden harp, so perfectly wrought that he no sooner held it than it seemed to play of itself.

"Take this, my sparrow," said Orddu, "and be the greatest bard in Prydain, known throughout the land for the beauty of your songs."

Dallben's heart leaped as the instrument thrilled in his arms. He touched the sweeping curve of the glowing harp and ran his fingers over the golden strings. "I have never heard such music," he murmured. "Who owns this will surely have no lack of fame."

"You'll have fame and admiration a-plenty," said Orddu, "as long as anyone remembers you."

"Alas, that's true," Orwen said with a sigh. "Memory can be so skimpy. It doesn't stretch very far; and, next thing you know, there's your fame gone all crumbly and mildewed."

Sadly, Dallben set down the harp. "Beautiful it is," he said, "but in the end, I fear, little help to me."

"There's nothing else we can offer at the moment," said Orddu, delving once more into the chest, "unless you'd care to have this book."

The enchantress held up a large, heavy tome and blew away the dust and cobwebs from its moldering leather binding. "It's a bulky thing for a young lamb to carry. Naturally, it would be rather weighty, for it holds everything that was ever known, is known, and will be known."

"It's full of wisdom, thick as oatmeal," added Orwen. "Quite scarce in the world—wisdom, not oatmeal—but that only makes it the more valuable."

"We have so many requests for other items," Orddu said. "Seven-league boots, cloaks of invisibility, and such great nonsense. For wisdom, practically none. Yet whoever owns this book shall have all that and more, if he likes. For the odd thing about wisdom is the more you use it the more it grows; and the more you share, the more you gain. You'd be amazed how few understand that. If they did, I suppose, they wouldn't need the book in the first place."

"Do you give this to me?" Dallben asked. "A treasure greater than all treasures?"

Orddu hesitated. "Give? Only in a manner of speaking. If you know us as well as you say you do, then you also know we don't exactly *give* anything. Put it this way: We shall *let* you take that heavy, dusty old book if that's what you truly want. Again, be warned: The greater the treasure, the greater the cost. Nothing is given for nothing; not in the Marshes of Morva—or anyplace else, for the matter of that."

"Even so," Dallben replied, "this book is my choice."

"Very well," said Orddu, putting the ancient volume in his hands. "Now you shall be on your way. We're sorry to see you go, though sorrow is something we don't usually feel. Fare well, dear chicken. We mean this in the polite sense, for whether you fare well or ill is entirely up to you."

So Dallben took his leave of the enchantresses and set off eagerly, curious to see what lay in store not only in the world but between the covers of the book. Once the cottage was well out of sight and the marshes far behind him, he curbed his impatience no longer, but sat down by the roadside, opened the heavy tome, and began to read.

As he scanned the first pages, his eyes widened and his heart quickened. For here was knowledge he had never dreamed of: the pathways of the stars, the rounds of the planets, the ebb and flow of time and tide. All secrets of the world and all its hidden lore unfolded to him.

Dallben's head spun, giddy with delight. The huge book seemed to weigh less than a feather, and he felt so lighthearted he could have skipped from one mountaintop to the next and never touched the ground. He laughed and sang at the top of his voice, bursting with gladness, pride, and strength in what he had learned.

"I chose well!" he cried, jumping to his feet. "But why should Orddu have warned me? Cost? What cost can there be? Knowledge is joy!"

He strode on, reading as he went. Each page lightened and sped his journey, and soon he came to a village where the dwellers danced and sang and made holiday. They offered him meat and drink and shelter for the coming night.

But Dallben thanked them for their hospitality and shook his head, saying he had meat and drink enough in the book he carried. By this time he had walked many miles, but his spirit was fresh and his legs unweary.

He kept on his way, hardly able to contain his happiness as he read and resolving not to rest until he had come to the end of the book. But he had finished less than half when the pages, to his horror, began to grow dark and stained with blood and tears.

For now the book told him of other ways of the world; of cruelty, suffering, and death. He read of greed, hatred, and war; of men striving against one another with fire and sword; of the blossoming earth trampled underfoot, of harvests lost and lives cut short. And the book told that even in the same village he had passed, a day would come when no house would stand; when women would weep for their men, and children for their parents; and where they had offered him meat and drink, they would starve for lack of a crust of bread.

Each page he read pierced his heart. The book, which had seemed to weigh so little, now grew so heavy that his pace faltered and he staggered under the burden. Tears blinded his eyes, and he stumbled to the ground.

All night he lay shattered by despair. At dawn he stirred and found it took all his efforts even to lift his head. Bones aching, throat parched, he crept on hands and knees to quench his thirst from a puddle of water. There, at the sight of his reflection, he drew back and cried out in anguish.

His fair, bright curls had gone frost-white and fell below his brittle shoulders. His cheeks, once full and flushed with youth, were now hollow and wrinkled, half hidden by a long, gray beard. His brow, smooth yesterday, was scarred and furrowed, his hands gnarled and knotted, his eyes pale as if their color had been wept away.

Dallben bowed his head. "Yes, Orddu," he whispered, "I should have heeded you. Nothing is given without cost. But is the cost of wisdom so high? I thought knowledge was joy. Instead, it is grief beyond bearing."

The book lay nearby. Its last pages were still unread and, for a moment, Dallben thought to tear them to shreds and scatter them to the wind. Then he said:

"I have begun it, and I will finish it, whatever else it may foretell."

Fearfully and reluctantly, he began to read once more. But now his heart lifted. These pages told not only of death, but of birth as well; how the earth turns in its own time and in its own way gives back what is given to it; how things lost may be found again; and how one day ends for another to begin. He learned that the lives of men are short and filled with pain, yet each one a priceless treasure, whether it be that of a prince or a pig-keeper. And, at the last, the book taught him that while nothing was certain, all was possible.

"At the end of knowledge, wisdom begins," Dallben murmured. "And at the end of wisdom there is not grief, but hope."

He climbed to his withered legs and hobbled along his way, clasping the heavy book. After a time a farmer drove by in a horse-drawn cart, and called out to him:

"Come, Grandfather, ride with me if you like. That book must be a terrible load for an old man like you."

"Thank you just the same," Dallben answered, "but I have strength enough now to go to the end of my road."

"And where might that be?"

"I do not know," Dallben said. "I go seeking it."

"Well, then," said the farmer, "may you be lucky enough to find it."

"Luck?" Dallben answered. He smiled and shook his head. "Not luck, but hope. Indeed, hope."

# The Stone

There was a cottager named Maibon, and one day he was driving down the road in his horse and cart when he saw an old man hobbling along, so frail and feeble he doubted the poor soul could go many more steps. Though Maibon offered to take him in the cart, the old man refused; and Maibon went his way home, shaking his head over such a pitiful sight, and said to his wife, Modrona:

"Ah, ah, what a sorry thing it is to have your bones creaking and cracking, and dim eyes, and dull wits. When I think this might come to me, too! A fine, strong-armed, sturdy-legged fellow like me? One day to go tottering, and have his teeth rattling in his head, and live on porridge, like a baby? There's no fate worse in all the world."

"There is," answered Modrona, "and that would be to have neither teeth nor porridge. Get on with you, Maibon, and stop borrowing trouble. Hoe your field or you'll have no crop to harvest, and no food for you, nor me, nor the little ones."

Sighing and grumbling, Maibon did as his wife bade him. Although the day was fair and cloudless, he took no pleasure in it. His axe-blade was notched, the wooden handle splintery; his saw had lost its edge; and his hoe, once shining new, had begun to rust. None of his tools, it seemed to him, cut or chopped or delved as well as they once had done.

"They're as worn out as that old codger I saw on the road," Maibon said to himself. He squinted up at the sky. "Even the sun isn't as bright as it used to be, and doesn't warm me half as well. It's gone threadbare as my cloak. And no wonder, for it's been there longer than I can remember. Come to think of it, the moon's been looking a little wilted around the edges, too.

"As for me," went on Maibon, in dismay, "I'm in even a worse state. My appetite's faded, especially after meals. Mornings, when I wake, I can hardly keep myself from yawning. And at night, when I go to bed, my eyes are so heavy I can't hold them open. If that's the way things are now, the older I grow, the worse it will be!"

In the midst of his complaining, Maibon glimpsed something bouncing and tossing back and forth beside a fallen tree in a corner of the field. Wondering if one of his piglets had squeezed out of the sty and gone rooting for acorns, Maibon hurried across the turf. Then he dropped his axe and gaped in astonishment.

There, struggling to free his leg which had been caught under the log, lay a short, thickset figure: a dwarf with red hair bristling in all directions beneath his round, close-fitting leather cap. At the sight of Maibon, the dwarf squeezed shut his bright red eyes and began holding his breath. After a moment, the dwarf's face went redder than his hair; his cheeks puffed out and soon turned purple. Then he opened one eye and blinked rapidly at Maibon, who was staring at him, speechless.

"What," snapped the dwarf, "you can still see me?"

"That I can," replied Maibon, more than ever puzzled, "and I can see very well you've got yourself tight as a wedge under that log, and all your kicking only makes it worse."

At this, the dwarf blew out his breath and shook his fists. "I can't do it!" he shouted. "No matter how I try! I can't make myself invisible! Everyone in my family can disappear—Poof! Gone! Vanished! But not me! Not Doli! Believe me, if I could have done, you never would have found me in such a plight. Worse luck! Well, come on. Don't stand there goggling like an idiot. Help me get loose!"

At this sharp command, Maibon began tugging and heaving at the log. Then he stopped, wrinkled his brow, and scratched his head, saying:

"Well, now, just a moment, friend. The way you look, and all your talk about turning yourself invisible—I'm thinking you might be one of the Fair Folk."

"Oh, clever!" Doli retorted. "Oh, brilliant! Great clodhopper! Giant beanpole! Of course I am! What else! Enough gabbling. Get a move on. My leg's going to sleep."

"If a man does the Fair Folk a good turn," cried Maibon, his excitement growing, "it's told they must do one for him."

"I knew sooner or later you'd come round to that," grumbled the dwarf. "That's the way of it with you ham-handed, heavy-footed oafs. Time was, you humans got along well with us. But nowadays, you no sooner see a Fair Folk than it's grab, grab, grab! Gobble, gobble, gobble! Grant my wish! Give me this, give me that! As if we had nothing better to do!

"Yes, I'll give you a favor," Doli went on. "That's the rule, I'm obliged to. Now, get on with it."

Hearing this, Maibon pulled and pried and chopped away at the log as fast as he could, and soon freed the dwarf.

Doli heaved a sigh of relief, rubbed his shin, and cocked a red eye at Maibon, saying:

"All right. You've done your work, you'll have your reward. What do you want? Gold, I suppose. That's the usual. Jewels? Fine clothes? Take my advice, go for something practical. A hazelwood twig to help you find water if your well ever goes dry? An axe that never needs sharpening? A cook-pot always brimming with food?"

"None of those!" cried Maibon. He bent down to the dwarf and whispered eagerly, "But I've heard tell that you Fair Folk have magic stones that can keep a man young forever. That's what I want. I claim one for my reward."

Doli snorted. "I might have known you'd pick something like that. As to be expected, you humans have it all muddled. There's nothing can make a man young again. That's even beyond the best of our skills. Those stones you're babbling about? Well, yes, there are such things. But greatly overrated. All they'll do is keep you from growing any older."

"Just as good!" Maibon exclaimed. "I want no more than that!"

Doli hesitated and frowned. "Ah—between the two of us, take the cook-pot. Better all around. Those stones—we'd sooner not give them away. There's a difficulty—"

"Because you'd rather keep them for yourselves," Maibon broke in. "No, no, you shan't cheat me of my due. Don't put me off with excuses. I told you what I want, and that's what I'll have. Come, hand it over and not another word."

Doli shrugged and opened a leather pouch that hung from his belt. He spilled a number of brightly colored pebbles into his palm, picked out one of the larger stones, and handed it to Maibon. The dwarf then jumped up, took to his heels, raced across the field, and disappeared into a thicket.

Laughing and crowing over his good fortune and his cleverness, Maibon hurried back to the cottage. There, he told his wife what had happened, and showed her the stone he had claimed from the Fair Folk.

"As I am now, so I'll always be!" Maibon declared, flexing his arms and thumping his chest. "A fine figure of a man! Oho, no gray beard and wrinkled brow for me!"

Instead of sharing her husband's jubilation, Modrona flung up her hands and burst out:

"Maibon, you're a greater fool than ever I supposed! And selfish into the bargain! You've turned down treasures! You didn't even ask that dwarf for so much as new jackets for the children! Nor a new apron for me! You could have had the roof mended. Or the walls plastered. No, a stone is what you ask for! A bit of rock no better than you'll dig up in the cow pasture!"

Crestfallen and sheepish, Maibon began thinking his wife was right, and the dwarf had indeed given him no more than a common field stone.

"Eh, well, it's true," he stammered, "I feel no different than I did this morning, no better nor worse, but every way the same. That redheaded little wretch! He'll rue the day if I ever find him again!"

So saying, Maibon threw the stone into the fireplace. That night he grumbled his way to bed, dreaming revenge on the dishonest dwarf.

Next morning, after a restless night, he yawned, rubbed his eyes, and scratched his chin. Then he sat bolt upright in bed, patting his cheeks in amazement.

"My beard!" he cried, tumbling out and hurrying to tell his wife. "It hasn't grown! Not by a hair! Can it be the dwarf didn't cheat me after all?"

"Don't talk to me about beards," declared his wife as Maibon went to the fireplace, picked out the stone, and clutched it safely in both hands. "There's trouble enough in the chicken roost. Those eggs should have hatched by now, but the hen is still brooding on her nest."

"Let the chickens worry about that," answered Maibon. "Wife, don't you see what a grand thing's happened to me? I'm not a minute older than I was yesterday. Bless that generous-hearted dwarf!"

"Let me lay hands on him and I'll bless him," retorted Modrona. "That's all well and good for you. But what of me? You'll stay as you are, but I'll turn old and gray, and worn and wrinkled, and go doddering into my grave! And what of our little ones? They'll grow up and have children of their own. And grandchildren, and great-grandchildren. And you, younger than any of them. What a foolish sight you'll be!"

But Maibon, gleeful over his good luck, paid his wife no heed, and only tucked the stone deeper into his pocket. Next day, however, the eggs had still not hatched.

"And the cow!" Modrona cried. "She's long past due to calve, and no sign of a young one ready to be born!"

"Don't bother me with cows and chickens," replied Maibon. "They'll all come right, in time. As for time, I've got all the time in the world!"

Having no appetite for breakfast, Maibon went out into his field. Of all the seeds he had sown there, however, he was surprised to see not one had sprouted. The field, which by now should have been covered with green shoots, lay bare and empty.

"Eh, things do seem a little late these days," Maibon said to himself. "Well, no hurry. It's that much less for me to do. The wheat isn't growing, but neither are the weeds."

Some days went by and still the eggs had not hatched, the cow had not calved, the wheat had not sprouted. And now Maibon saw that his apple tree showed no sign of even the smallest, greenest fruit.

"Maibon, it's the fault of that stone!" wailed his wife. "Get rid of the thing!"

"Nonsense," replied Maibon. "The season's slow, that's all."

Nevertheless, his wife kept at him and kept at him so much that Maibon at last, and very reluctantly, threw the stone out of the cottage window. Not too far, though, for he had it in the back of his mind to go later and find it again.

Next morning he had no need to go looking for it, for there was the stone sitting on the window ledge.

"You see?" said Maibon to his wife. "Here it is back again. So, it's a gift meant for me to keep."

"Maibon!" cried his wife. "Will you get rid of it! We've had nothing but trouble since you brought it into the house. Now the baby's fretting and fuming. Teething, poor little thing. But not a tooth to be seen! Maibon, that stone's bad luck and I want no part of it!"

Protesting it was none of his doing that the stone had come back, Maibon carried it into the vegetable patch. He dug a hole, not a very deep one, and put the stone into it.

Next day, there was the stone above ground, winking and glittering.

"Maibon!" cried his wife. "Once and for all, if you care for your family, get rid of that cursed thing!"

Seeing no other way to keep peace in the household, Maibon regretfully and unwillingly took the stone and threw it down the well, where it splashed into the water and sank from sight.

But that night, while he was trying vainly to sleep, there came such a rattling and clattering that Maibon clapped his hands over his ears, jumped out of bed, and went stumbling into the yard. At the well, the bucket was jiggling back and forth and up and down at the end of the rope; and in the bottom of the bucket was the stone.

Now Maibon began to be truly distressed, not only for the toothless baby, the calfless cow, the fruitless tree, and the hen sitting desperately on her eggs, but for himself as well.

"Nothing's moving along as it should," he groaned. "I can't tell one day from another. Nothing changes, there's nothing to look forward to, nothing to show for my work. Why sow if the seeds don't sprout? Why plant if there's never a harvest? Why eat if I don't get hungry? Why go to bed at night, or get up in the morning, or do anything at all? And the way it looks, so it will stay forever and ever! I'll shrivel from boredom if nothing else!"

"Maibon," pleaded his wife, "for all our sakes, destroy the dreadful thing!"

Maibon tried now to pound the stone to dust with his heaviest mallet; but he could not so much as knock a chip from it. He put it against his grindstone without so much as scratching it. He set it on his anvil and belabored it with hammer and tongs, all to no avail.

At last he decided to bury the stone again, this time deeper than before. Picking up his shovel, he hurried to the field. But he suddenly halted and the shovel dropped from his hands. There, sitting cross-legged on a stump, was the dwarf.

"You!" shouted Maibon, shaking his fist. "Cheat! Villain! Trickster! I did you a good turn, and see how you've repaid it!"

The dwarf blinked at the furious Maibon. "You mortals are an ungrateful crew. I gave you what you wanted."

"You should have warned me!" burst out Maibon.

"I did," Doli snapped back. "You wouldn't listen. No, you yapped and yammered, bound to have your way. I told you we didn't like to give away those stones. When you mortals get hold of one, you stay just as you are—but so does everything around you. Before you know it, you're mired in time like a rock in the mud. You take my advice. Get rid of that stone as fast as you can."

"What do you think I've been trying to do?" blurted Maibon. "I've buried it, thrown it down the well, pounded it with a hammer—it keeps coming back to me!"

"That's because you really didn't want to give it up," Doli said. "In the back of your mind and the bottom of your heart, you didn't want to change along with the rest of the world. So long as you feel that way, the stone is yours."

"No, no!" cried Maibon. "I want no more of it. Whatever may happen, let it happen. That's better than nothing happening at all. I've had my share of being young, I'll take my share of being old. And when I come to the end of my days, at least I can say I've lived each one of them."

"If you mean that," answered Doli, "toss the stone onto the ground, right there at the stump. Then get home and be about your business."

Maibon flung down the stone, spun around, and set off as fast as he could. When he dared at last to glance back over his shoulder, fearful the stone might be bouncing along at his heels, he saw no sign of it, nor of the redheaded dwarf.

Maibon gave a joyful cry, for at that same instant the fallow field was covered with green blades of wheat, the branches of the apple tree bent to the ground, so laden they were with fruit. He ran to the cottage, threw his arms around his wife and children, and told them the good news. The hen hatched her chicks, the cow bore her calf. And Maibon laughed with glee when he saw the first tooth in the baby's mouth.

Never again did Maibon meet any of the Fair Folk, and he was just as glad of it. He and his wife and children and grandchildren lived many years, and Maibon was proud of his white hair and long beard as he had been of his sturdy arms and legs.

"Stones are all right, in their way," said Maibon. "But the trouble with them is, they don't grow."

# The True Enchanter

When Princess Angharad of the Royal House of Llyr came of an age to be married, her mother, Queen Regat, sent throughout the kingdom to find suitors for her daughter's hand. With red-gold hair and sea-green eyes, Angharad was the most beautiful of all the princesses of Llyr; and there were many who would have courted her. However, because Angharad was an enchantress of long and lofty lineage, it was forbidden her to wed any but an enchanter.

"That," said Angharad, "is the most ridiculous rule I've ever heard of. It's vexing enough, having to curtsy here, curtsy there, smile when you'd rather frown, frown when you'd rather laugh, and look interested when you're actually bored to tears. And now, is my husband to be chosen for me?"

"Rules are to be obeyed, not questioned," answered Queen Regat. "You may wed the one your heart desires, and choose your husband freely—among those, naturally, with suitable qualifications."

"It seems to me," said Angharad, "one of the qualifications should be that we love each other."

"Desirable," said Queen Regat, "but in matters of state, not always practical."

And so Queen Regat commanded that only enchanters of the highest skill should present themselves in turn at the Great Hall of the Castle of Llyr.

First came the enchanter Gildas. He was paunchy, with fleshy cheeks shining as if buttered. His garments were embroidered with gold thread and crusted with jewels. The host of servants following in his train were garbed almost as splendidly as their master; and, at the sight, murmurs of admiration rose from all the courtiers. Nose in the air, looking neither right nor left, Gildas bustled through the Great Hall to stand before the thrones of Angharad and her mother, and curtly nodded his balding head.

"Noblest ladies," Gildas began, "allow me to dispense with the formalities. You appreciate the demands upon my time. Only with greatest difficulty have I been able to spare a few moments from an especially busy morning. Therefore, I trust we may promptly negotiate, determine, and settle upon the nuptial agreements; and, of primary consideration and concern, the question of dowry, the pecuniary contribution, the treasure the Princess brings as her marriage portion."

"What?" burst out Angharad, before her mother could reply. "Prompt? Pecuniary? Settlement? You're a good step ahead of yourself, Master Gildas. If I'm obliged to marry an enchanter, I'd first like to see some enchantments. Then I'll make up my own mind."

"My dear young girl," Gildas haughtily replied, "there is no reason to waste time in trivial details. Surely my reputation has preceded me. My skill is beyond question, I have impeccable recommendations."

"And a wonderful opinion of yourself—well earned, no doubt," Angharad said sweetly. "Do allow us to share it. Favor us with a demonstration."

Sniffing and sputtering, Gildas could only do as he was requested. Impatiently, he snapped his fingers, commanding a servant to bring a long cloak, even more dazzling than his other garments, and to drape it over his shoulders. Gildas then commanded another to bring a tall, pointed headpiece covered with magical signs; and a third to fetch a long golden staff.

Thus arrayed, Gildas began mumbling and muttering, and with his staff, tracing patterns on the flagstones. Puffing from his exertions, the enchanter circled first in one direction, then another, droning spells, waving his arms, and waggling his fingers.

Through all this, Princess Angharad tapped her foot, drummed her fingers on the arm of the throne, and stared out the casement. Even Queen Regat could not hide the frown that shadowed her usually composed features.

Gildas kept on with his laborious incantations for some time, until his brow glistened and he was out of breath. At last a small gray cloud began taking shape in the air. The enchanter doubled his efforts, flapping his arms and gesturing as if he were kneading a basin of dough. Little by little the cloud grew bigger and blacker until it filled the Great Hall. The shadows deepened and thickened, blotting out the sunlight from the casements, and the Great Hall was dark as midnight.

The courtiers and royal retainers whispered their amazement at such a feat. Gildas clapped his hands sharply; the cloud broke into fragments, the blackness seeped away, and the Great Hall was bright as it had been before.

The enchanter mopped his streaming brow. His cheeks flushed as he smiled with self-satisfaction. Queen Regat nodded in recognition of his prowess. Princess Angharad stifled a yawn.

"Well?" said Angharad.

Gildas blinked at her. "I beg your pardon?"

"Is that all there is to it?" Angharad asked. "Is this the enchantment you offer us?"

"All there is?" exclaimed Gildas. "One of my finest effects! My dear Princess—"

"My dear enchanter," Angharad replied, "I don't doubt for a moment you've gone to a great deal of work and strain. I only hope you haven't done yourself harm. Not to say anything against your spells, you understand, but frankly, I don't see the point of going to such trouble for the sake of turning day into night. All anybody needs to do is be patient a little while and night will come along very nicely by itself, with a far better quality of darkness than yours—much more velvety. Not to mention the moon and a whole skyful of stars for good measure."

"Then, Princess," returned Gildas, taken aback, "allow me to produce something a little more spectacular. I suggest a snowstorm. My blizzards never fail to please, they have always been received with approbation."

Angharad sighed and shrugged. "There again, Master Gildas, why bother? When the proper season comes round, we'll have snow enough; each flake different, too. Can you do as well?"

Sputtering and stammering, Gildas admitted he could not. "But—but, perhaps, a culinary manifestation, a full-course feast? Roast goose? Wine? Sweetmeats?"

"We're quite satisfied with our own cook," said Angharad. "Thank you, no."

Scowling in wounded dignity, grumbling at the disrespect of young princesses, Gildas seated himself beside Queen Regat, awaiting the next suitor.

"It is against my principles to criticize my colleagues," he muttered to the Queen. "But I can assure Your Majesty in advance: No enchantments can rival mine."

Queen Regat nevertheless beckoned for the second suitor to enter the Great Hall. This was the enchanter Grimgower, lean, gaunt-faced, with knotted brows and a square black beard twining around his thin lips. His iron-shod boots rang as he strode toward the thrones, and his black cloak streamed behind him. In his train marched dark-robed, hooded servants, and the courtiers drew back uneasily as they passed.

Grimgower halted before Angharad, folded his arms, and threw back his head.

"Princess," he said, "I come to claim your hand and declare myself willing to accept you as my wife."

"At least," replied Angharad, "that settles half the question."

"Let us understand each other," said Grimgower. "The House of Llyr is known for the powers of enchantresses. And the willfulness of its daughters. You shall have all you wish, and more. No luxury will be denied you. But in my household, I am the only master."

"You make it sound delightful," said Angharad.

"Think more of your duty and less of your pleasure," Grimgower answered. "The sons born of our marriage will have powers beyond all others and will rule supreme throughout the land. The joining of our two houses—"

"It's not houses getting married, it's me," said Angharad. "And if you can tell ahead of time that you'll have sons instead of daughters you're a prophet, indeed! Meanwhile, I suggest that you demonstrate your skill in some other way."

Grimgower stepped back a pace and raised his arms. In a harsh voice he called out the words of a mighty enchantment. The courtiers gasped in terror. For now, out of thin air, suddenly sprang monstrous creatures that snarled, bared sharp fangs, and snapped their jaws. Some, covered with scales, breathed fire through their nostrils; others lashed tails as sharp as swords. The beasts crouched beside the enchanter and glared with blazing eyes at Angharad.

Queen Regat paled, though she sat stiff and straight and tried to conceal her alarm.

Angharad, however, glanced unperturbed at the monsters.

"Poor things, they looked starved for their dinner," she said to Grimgower. "You should really take better care of them. They need a good brushing and combing, too. I daresay they're all flea-ridden."

"These are no common enchantments," cried Grimgower, his face twisting angrily, "but creatures shaped of my own dreams. I alone can summon them. You shall not see their like in all the realm."

"Happily," said Angharad. "Yes, I suppose they would be the sort of things you, Master Grimgower, would dream of, and no doubt you're proud of them. I hope you won't be offended if I tell you honestly I prefer the animals we have in our forest. The deer are much handsomer than that dismal-looking whatever-it-is next to you. So are the rabbits, the badgers, and all the others. And I'm sure they have better tempers."

Frowning darkly, Grimgower spread his cloak, spat an incantation through his clenched teeth, and the monstrous beings disappeared as quickly as they had come. At a sign from Queen Regat, the enchanter took his place beside Gildas, and the two rivals looked daggers at each other.

"So far," Angharad whispered to her mother, "the choice is easy. Neither! Are there no other suitors? It's not that I expect a crowd, all jostling and clamoring to marry me, but I'd really hate to think only two were interested, especially those two."

"Alas, daughter, there are none," Queen Regat began, but

stopped as the Chief Steward came to murmur a few words in her ear. Queen Regat turned to Angharad and said:

"One more awaits. Geraint is his name. He is unknown to me, but he asks admittance to seek your hand."

Angharad shrugged and sighed wearily. "I've put up with this pair. I doubt a third could be more tiresome."

But the Princess caught her breath as the enchanter Geraint made his way through the Great Hall and stood before her. He came with no servants or attendants; he bore no magic wand or golden staff; his garments were plain and unadorned. Yet this youth was the fairest Angharad had ever seen. Nevertheless, despite her quickening heart and the color rising to her cheeks, she tossed her head and said lightly:

"Now, Master Geraint, by what enchantments do you mean to court us?"

Geraint smiled as he replied.

"Why, Princess, by none at all. Does a man court a woman with sorcery? It seems to me he must court her with love."

"Boldly spoken," said Angharad, "but how shall you do so?"

"As a man to a woman," answered Geraint. "And may you answer me freely, as a woman to a man."

As their eyes met, Angharad knew her heart could be given only to him. However, before she could reply, the enchanter Gildas stepped forward, sputtering and protesting. And the enchanter Grimgower sprang from his seat and angrily insisted that Geraint prove his skill, as they had been obliged to do.

And so Geraint began. However, unlike the others, he drew no magical patterns, pronounced no magical spells. Instead, in common, quiet words he spoke of waters and woodlands, of sea and sky, of men and women, of childhood and old age; of the wonder and beauty of living things, all closely woven one with the other as threads on the same loom.

As he spoke, he stretched out his open hands, and all in the court fell silent, marveling. For now, born of his simple gesture, appeared flights of doves, fluttering and circling around him. Flowers blossomed at each motion of his fingers. He raised his arms and above his head stars glittered in a sparkling cloud and a shower of lights was scattered through the Great Hall.

Then Geraint lowered his arms to his sides, and the enchantments vanished. He stood waiting, saying nothing more, while his glance and the glance of Angharad touched and held each other. Smiling, the Princess rose from her throne.

"My choice is made," she said. "The enchanter Geraint has sought my hand and won my heart. And so shall we be wed."

Shouts of joy filled the Great Hall as Angharad and Geraint stepped forward to embrace.

But Grimgower thrust himself between them. His face was livid with rage as he cried out to Queen Regat and all the company:

"What trickery is this? He used no sorcery known to me or to any magician. He is an impostor! A false enchanter! Cast him out!"

"He has tried to dupe us," fumed Gildas, his jowls shaking with indignation. "My colleague is correct. I heard no proper spells or charms. This upstart has no true power. A hoaxer! A mere juggler!"

Angharad was about to protest, but the Queen gestured for her to be silent. Regat's face was grave as she drew herself up and turned a severe gaze upon Geraint.

"You have heard these accusations," Queen Regat said. "Are they true?"

"Yes," Geraint answered willingly, "altogether true. Sorcery is not my birthright. I have no inborn powers. What I showed, I fashioned by myself. The birds you saw? No doves, but only bits of white parchment. The flowers? Dry grass and tinted leaves. The stars? A handful of bright pebbles. I only helped you imagine these things to be more than what they are. If this pleased you for a few moments, I could ask nothing better."

"How dare you come to us in the guise of an enchanter?" demanded the Queen.

"To win Angharad's hand," replied Geraint, "I would dare more than that."

"Even so," answered the Queen. "My daughter has chosen you in vain."

"No!" declared Angharad. "Any other choice would be in vain. Those two inherited their skills. Geraint earned his. False? He's the only true enchanter."

"Perhaps you are right," Queen Regat answered. She sighed and shook her head. "Daughter, though I wish your happiness, by rule and custom your marriage to him is forbidden."

Since Angharad would consent to none but Geraint, the Queen regretfully commanded the Princess to withdraw and remain in her chambers. And Geraint was sent from the Castle of Llyr.

But Angharad defied the ancient rule and followed Geraint, and found him waiting for her as if each had known the other's mind.

As the two made their way through the forest beyond the castle, suddenly the sky grew dark as midnight, though the day was barely past high noon. But, from her cloak, Angharad drew a golden sphere which glowed at her touch and whose light overcame this vengeful sorcery of Gildas.

Then, in front of Angharad and Geraint sprang monstrous

creatures summoned by Grimgower. But the two clasped hands and kept on their way. And the creatures drew back and bowed their heads while the lovers passed unharmed.

At the edge of the forest a thick curtain of snow began to fall, and icy gales lashed Angharad and Geraint. But they held each other closer and so passed through it, too, in warmth and safety.

And where they left footprints in the snow, flowers bloomed.

# The Rascal Crow

Medwyn, ancient guardian and protector of animals, one day sent urgent word for the birds and beasts to join in council with him. So from lair and burrow, nest and hive, proud stag and humble mole, bright-winged eagle and drab wren, they hastened to his valley. No human could have found or followed the secret path to this shelter, for only creatures of field and forest had knowledge of it.

There they gathered, every kind and degree, one from each clan and tribe. Before them stood Medwyn garbed in a coarse brown robe, his white beard reaching to his waist, his white hair about his shoulders, his only ornament a golden band, set with a blue gem, circling his weathered brow. He spread his gnarled and knotted arms in welcome to the waiting council.

"You know, all of you," he began, in a clear voice unweakened by his years, "long ago, when the dark waters flooded Prydain, I built a ship and carried your forefathers here to safety. Now I must warn you: your own lives are threatened."

Hearing this, the animals murmured and twittered in dismay. But Kadwyr the crow flapped his glossy wings, clacked his beak, and gaily called out:

"What, more wind and water? Let the ducks have the joy of it! Don't worry about me. My nest is high and strong enough. I'll stay where I am. Good sailing to all web-feet!"

Chuckling, making loud, impudent quackings at the blue teal, Kadwyr would have flown off then and there. Medwyn summoned him back, saying:

"Ah, Kadwyr, you're as great a scamp as your grandsire who sailed with me. No, it is neither flood nor storm. The danger is far worse. King Arawn, Lord of the Land of Death, seeks to enslave all you forest creatures, to break you to his will and bind you to serve his evil ends. Those cousins to the eagles, the gentle gwythaints, have already fallen prey to him. Arawn has lured them to his realm and trapped them in iron cages. Alas, they are beyond our help. We can only grieve for them.

"Take warning from their fate," Medwyn continued. "For now the Death-Lord sends his Chief Huntsman to bait and snare you, to bring you captive to the Land of Death or to slaughter you without mercy. Together you must set your plans to stand against him."

"A crow's a match for any hunter," said Kadwyr. "Watch your step, the rest of you, especially you slow-footed cud-chewers."

Medwyn sighed and shook his head at the brash crow. "Even you, Kadwyr, may be glad for another's help."

Kadwyr only shrugged his wings and cocked a bold eye at Edyrnion the eagle, who flew to perch on Medwyn's outstretched arm.

"Friend of eagles," Edyrnion said, "I and my kinsmen will keep watch from the sky. Our eyes are keen, our wings are swift. At first sight of the hunter, we will spread the alarm."

"Mind you, don't fly too close to the sun," put in Kadwyr with a raucous chuckle. "You'll singe your pinfeathers and moult ahead of season. If there's any watching needed, I'd best be the one to do it. I hear you're going a bit nearsighted these days."

The nimble crow hopped away before the eagle could call him to account for his teasing. And now the gray wolf Brynach came to crouch at Medwyn's feet, saying:

"Friend of wolves, I and my kinsmen will range the forest. Our teeth are sharp, our jaws are strong. Should the hunter come among us, let him beware of our wolf packs."

"And you'd better watch out for that long tail of yours," said Kadwyr. "With all your dashing back and forth, you're likely to get burrs in it. In fact, you might do well to leave all that roving and roaming to me. My beak's as sharp as any wolf's tooth. And," the crow added, winking, "I never have to stop and scratch fleas."

The wolf's golden eyes flashed and he looked ready to teach the crow a lesson in manners. But he kept his temper and sat back on his haunches as Gwybeddin the gnat flew close to Medwyn's ear and bravely piped up:

"Friend of gnats! We are a tiny folk, but we mean to do our best in any way we can."

Hearing this, Kadwyr squawked with laughter and called out to the gnat:

"Is that you, Prince Flyspeck? I can hardly see you. Listen, old friend, the best thing you can do is hide in a dust cloud, and no hunter will ever find you. Why, even your words are bigger than you are!"

Kadwyr's remarks so embarrassed the poor gnat that he blushed and buzzed away as fast as he could. Meantime, Nedir the spider had clambered up to Medwyn's sleeve, where she clung with her long legs, and declared:

"Friend of spiders! We spinners and weavers are craftsmen, not fighters. But we shall give our help gladly wherever it is needed."

"Take my advice, Granny," Kadwyr said with a chuckle, "and

keep to your knitting. Be careful you don't get your arms and legs mixed up, or you'll never untangle them."

Kadwyr hopped about and flirted his tailfeathers, croaking and cackling as the other creatures came forward one by one. The owl declared that he and his fellows would serve as night watch. The fox vowed to use his cunning to baffle the hunter and lead him on false trails. The bees pledged to wield their stings as swords and daggers. The bears offered their strength, the stags their speed, and the badgers their courage to protect their neighbors and themselves.

Last of all, plodding under his heavy burden, came Crugan-Crawgan the turtle.

"Friend of turtles," began Crugan-Crawgan in a halting voice, pondering each word, "I came . . . yes, well, that is to say I, ah, started . . . in all possible haste . . ."

"And we'll be well into next week by the time you're done telling us," Kadwyr said impatiently.

"We are . . . as I should be the first to admit . . . we are, alas, neither swift nor strong. But if I might be allowed . . . ah, permitted to state . . . we're solid. Very, very . . . solid. And . . . steady."

"Have done!" cried Kadwyr, hopping onto the turtle's shell. "You'll put me to sleep! The safest thing you can do is stay locked up in that portable castle of yours. Pull in your head! Tuck in your tail! I'll see to it the hunter doesn't batter down your walls. By the way, old fellow, didn't you have a race with a snail the other day? Tell me, who won?"

"Oh, that," replied Crugan-Crawgan. "Yes, Kadwyr, you see, what happened . . ."

Kadwyr did not wait for the turtle's answer, for Medwyn now declared the council ended, and the crow flapped away, laughing and cackling to himself. "Gnats and spiders! Turtles! What an army! I'll have to keep an eye on all of them."

Once in the forest, Kadwyr gave little thought to Medwyn's warning. The beavers toiled at making their dams into strongholds; the squirrels stopped up the crannies in their hollow trees; the moles dug deeper tunnels and galleries. Though every creature offered him shelter in case of need, Kadwyr shook his glossy head and answered:

"Not for me, those holes and burrows! Wits and wings! Wings and wits! There's not a crow hatched who can't get the best of any hunter!"

Soon Edyrnion and his eagle kinsmen came swooping into the forest, beating their wings and spreading the alarm. The wolf packs leaped from their lairs, the bears from their dens, the foxes from their earths, gathering to join battle against the hunter; and all the forest dwellers, each in his own way, made ready to defend nest and bower, cave and covert.

Kadwyr, however, perched on a branch, rocking back and forth, whistling gaily, daring the invader to catch him. While the smaller, weaker animals hid silent and fearful, Kadwyr hopped up and down, cawing at the top of his voice. And before the crow knew it, the hunter sprang from a thicket.

Garbed in the skins of slain animals, a long knife at his belt, a bow and quiver of arrows slung over his shoulder, the hunter had come so stealthily that Kadwyr scarcely had a moment to collect his wits. The hunter flung out a net so strong and finely woven that once caught in it, no creature could hope to struggle free.

But Kadwyr's eye was quicker than the hunter's snare. With a taunting cackle the crow hopped into the air, flapped his wings, and flew from the branch to perch higher in the tree, where he peered down and brazenly waggled his tailfeathers.

Leaving his net, with a snarl of anger the hunter unslung his bow, fitted an arrow to the string, and sent the shaft hissing straight for the crow.

Chuckling, Kadwyr fluttered his wings and sailed out of the path of the speeding arrow; then turned back to dance in the air in front of the furious hunter, who drew the bow again and again. Swooping and soaring, the crow dodged every shaft.

Seeing the hunter's quiver almost empty, Kadwyr grew even bolder, gliding closer, circling beyond reach, then swooping back to liven the game again. Gnashing his teeth at the elusive prey, the hunter struck out wildly, trying to seize the nimble crow.

Kadwyr sped away. As he flew, he turned his head in a backward glance to jeer at his defeated pursuer. In that heedless instant, the crow collided with a tree trunk.

Stunned, Kadwyr plummeted to the ground. The hunter ran toward him. Kadwyr croaked in pain as he strove to fly to safety. But his wing hung useless at his side, broken.

Breathless, Kadwyr scrambled into the bushes. The hunter plunged after him. Earthbound and wounded, Kadwyr began wishing he had not been so quick to turn down shelter from the squirrels and beavers. With the hunter gaining on him, the crow gladly would have squeezed into any tunnel, or burrow, or rabbit hole he could find. But all had been sealed, blocked, and barred with stones and twigs.

Dragging his wing, the crow skittered through the underbrush. His spindly legs were ill-suited to running, and he longed for the swiftness of the hare. He stumbled and went sprawling. An arrow buried itself in the ground beside him.

The hunter drew his bow. Though this was his pursuer's last arrow, Kadwyr knew himself a hopeless target. Only a few paces away, the hunter took aim.

The same instant, a cloud of dust came whirling through the trees. Expecting in another moment to be skewered, Kadwyr now saw the hunter fling up his arms and drop his bow. The arrow clattered harmlessly into the leaves. Next, Kadwyr was sure his opponent had lost his wits. Roaring with pain, the hunter waved his arms and beat his hands against his face, trying to fend off the cloud buzzing about his head and shoulders.

The host of gnats swarmed over the raging hunter, darted into his ears and eyes, streamed up his nose and out his mouth. The more the hunter swept away the tiny creatures, the more they set upon him.

"Gwybeddin!" burst out the crow as one of the swarm broke from the cloud and lit on his beak. "Thank you for my life! Did I call you a flyspeck? You and your gnats are as brave as eagles!"

"Hurry!" piped the gnat. "We're doing all we can, but he's more than a match for us. Quick, away with you!"

Kadwyr needed no urging. The gnats had saved him from the hunter's arrows and, as well, had let him snatch a moment's rest. The crow set off again as fast as he could scramble through the dry leaves and dead branches of the forest floor.

Brave though Gwybeddin and his fellows had been, their efforts did not keep the hunter long from the chase. Soon Kadwyr heard footfalls crashing close behind him. The hunter had easily found the crow's trail and seemed to gain in strength while his prey weakened with each step.

The crow plunged deeper into the woods, hoping to hide in a heavy growth of brambles or a thicket where the hunter could not follow. Instead, to Kadwyr's dismay, the forest here grew sparser. Before the crow could find cover, the hunter sighted him and gave a triumphant shout.

Not daring another backward glance, Kadwyr scrambled through a grove of trees. The ground before him lay clear and hard-packed; but while the way was easier for him, he realized it was easier, too, for his enemy to overtake him.

Just then Kadwyr heard a bellow of rage. The crow halted to see the hunter twisting and turning, struggling as if caught in his own net. Kadwyr stared in amazement. Amid the trees, Nedir and all the spiders in the forest had joined to spin their strongest webs. The strands were so fine the hunter had not seen them, but now they clung to him, twined and wrapped around him, and the more he tried to fight loose, the more they enshrouded him.

From a branch above Kadwyr's head, sliding down a single invisible thread, came Nedir, waving her long legs.

"We spinners and weavers have done our best," she called out, "but even our stoutest webs will soon give way. Be off, while you have a chance!"

"Granny spider," cried Kadwyr, "forgive me if I ever made sport of you. Your knitting saved my neck!"

Once again the crow scurried away, sure this time he had escaped for good and all. Despite the pain in his wing, his spirits rose and he began gleefully cackling at the sight of the hunter so enmeshed in a huge cocoon.

But Kadwyr soon snapped his beak shut. His eyes darted about in alarm, for his flight had brought him to the edge of a steep cliff.

He halted and fearfully drew back. Without the use of his wing he would have fallen like a stone and been dashed to pieces on the rocks below. However, before he could decide which way to turn, he saw the hunter racing toward him.

Free of the spiders' webs, more enraged than ever, and bent on making an end of the elusive crow, the hunter pulled his knife from his belt. With a shout of triumph, he sprang at the helpless Kadwyr.

The crow, certain his last moment had come, flapped his one good wing and thrust out his beak, bound that he would sell his life dearly.

But the hunter stumbled in mid-stride. His foot caught on a round stone that tripped him up and sent him plunging headlong over the cliff.

Kadwyr's terror turned to joyous relief. He cawed, cackled, and crowed as loudly as any rooster. Then his beak fell open in astonishment.

The stone that had saved his life began to sprout four stubby legs and a tail, a leathery neck stretched out cautiously, and Crugan-Crawgan, the turtle, blinked at Kadwyr.

"Are you all right?" asked Crugan-Crawgan. "That is, I mean to say . . . you've come to no harm? I'm sorry . . . ah, Kadwyr, there wasn't more I could have . . . done. We turtles, alas, can't run . . . like rabbits. Or fly . . . like eagles. But we are, I hope you'll agree . . . yes, we are solid, if nothing else. And . . . very, very steady."

"Crugan-Crawgan," said Kadwyr, "you saved my life and I thank you. Steady and solid you are, old fellow, and I'm glad of it."

"By the way," the turtle went on, "as I was saying . . . the last time we met . . . yes, the snail and I did have a race. It was . . . a draw."

The forest was again safe and the rejoicing animals came out of their hiding places. Edyrnion the eagle bore the wounded crow to Medwyn's valley, to be cared for and sheltered until his wing healed.

"Ah, Kadwyr, you scamp, I didn't expect to see you here so soon," Medwyn told the crow, who admitted all that had happened in the woods. "Your wing will mend and you'll be ready for some new scrape. But let us hope next time you can help your friends as they helped you."

"I know better than to scorn a spider," said Kadwyr, crestfallen. "I'll never taunt a turtle. And never again annoy a gnat. But—but, come to think of it," he went on, his eyes brightening, "if it hadn't been for me—yes, it was I! I who led that hunter a merry chase! I who saved all in the forest!"

Kadwyr chuckled and clucked, bobbed his head, and snapped his beak, altogether delighted with himself.

"Perhaps you did, at that," Medwyn gently answered. "In any case, go in peace, Kadwyr. The world has room enough for a rascal crow."

# The Sword

When Rhitta was crowned King of Prydain, the great sword Dyrnwyn, fairest ever wrought, was given him in token of his kingship. Its hilt was gem-studded, its blade forged in a secret way of which the knowledge had been long lost. On its scabbard were graven these words: *Draw Dyrnwyn, only thou of noble worth, to rule with justice, to strike down evil. Who wields it in good cause shall slay even the Lord of Death.* Of Dyrnwyn's lore and lineage little was known. King Rhydderch Hael, sire of King Rhych, and grandsire of Rhitta, had been the first to bear it, and it was said a deep enchantment had been laid upon it. So Rhitta, in his turn, bore Dyrnwyn as a weapon of power and protection over the land.

One day Rhitta and his nobles rode to the hunt. In the heat of the chase, Rhitta galloped across the field of the old shepherd, Amrys, and by mishap broke the gate of his sheepfold.

In dismay, Amrys called out to Rhitta:

"King, I pray you, mend my gate. My arms are too weak, my hands tremble, and I have no strength to set new posts and raise it again."

In his eagerness to follow the chase, Rhitta hastily answered:

"Shepherd, this is a small matter. You have my word it will be made right."

With that, seeing his nobles had gone on ahead, Rhitta spurred his horse after them. All day he hunted and at nightfall rode back weary to his castle. There his councilors awaited him with such pressing business and so many urgent questions that he forgot his promise to the shepherd.

Next morning, however, as Rhitta rode out hawking, at the portal stood the shepherd holding a young lamb in his arms.

"King, mend my gate," cried Amrys, clutching Rhitta's stirrup. "Already my sheep have strayed, all but this one lamb."

"Have I not given you my word?" answered Rhitta sharply, angry with himself at forgetting, but angrier still that the shepherd dared reproach him before his nobles. "Yours are small cares and will be set right in good time. Trouble me no longer with them."

The hawk on the King's wrist beat her wings impatiently. Rhitta kicked his stirrup free of the shepherd's hand, shouted for his hunting band to follow, and galloped on his way.

That night, with plates filled and wine flowing, Rhitta feasted in his Great Hall. Amid the laughter and boasting of his warriors and the music of his harpers, Rhitta had no thoughts for his promise to the shepherd.

Next day, Rhitta held court with all his councilors and his warleader to consider matters of policy and high state. In the midst of the council, pulling free of the guards who tried to hold him back, Amrys hobbled into the throne room and fell on his knees before the King.

"King, mend my gate," he cried, holding out the body of the lamb. "I have honored you as a worthy king and upright man, but now my sheep are lost and, for want of its mother, my lamb is dead."

"Shepherd," warned Rhitta, "I commanded you to trouble me no more. How dare you come into my council? Grave affairs are being weighed here."

"Sire," answered the shepherd, "is it not a grave thing when a king's promise goes unkept?"

"What, shepherd," Rhitta burst out, "do you tell me I have been false to my word?"

"No, sire," the shepherd returned simply, "I only tell you that so far it has not been kept."

Rhitta's face reddened at being so reproved, and he rose angrily from his throne to answer:

"Shepherd, mind your tongue! Do you call your king an oath-breaker?"

"You say it, sire, not I," replied Amrys.

These words of the shepherd so kindled his wrath that Rhitta drew his great sword and struck down Amrys. But then, when his rage lifted and he saw he had slain the old man, Rhitta was filled with remorse; he flung aside the weapon and covered his face with his hands.

However, his councilors gathered around him and said:

"Sire, that was a grievous deed. Nevertheless, the shepherd brought it on himself. He gave you a mortal insult, calling you a liar to your face. This affront to Your Majesty could have grown to treason and open rebellion. You could have done nothing else."

At first Rhitta had blamed only himself, but the more his councilors spoke, the more their words eased his mind and he saw the matter in their light. So, putting aside his regrets, he willingly agreed:

"Yes, it is true and clear to me now. I did only my duty. Even so, to show I bear no grudge, see to it the shepherd's wife and family are given each a purse filled with gold and the finest ram and ewe of my own flock; and never are they to want for anything whatsoever."

All the court hailed Rhitta's wisdom and generosity. But that night in his bed chamber, when he laid aside his weapons, on the bright scabbard of Dyrnwyn he saw a dark stain, the black of dried blood. Try as he would to wipe the scabbard clean, the dark stain remained.

Next day, his Chief Councilor came and told him:

"Sire, we would have done your bidding, but the shepherd has neither wife nor family. Indeed, he has no kindred to inherit his land."

Rhitta's war-leader, hearing this, came forward and said to the King:

"Sire, it has been your custom to reward those who serve you well. Before, when land was left without an heir, you bestowed it on other lords. Will you give this holding to me?"

Rhitta hesitated, weighing the war-leader's request but thinking, too, how well the shepherd's land would increase his own domains. Then he said:

"The shepherd affronted me. It is only justice that his land be added to mine."

"Justice?" retorted the war-leader. "The King's justice well serves the King's ends."

Rhitta turned angrily upon him and exclaimed:

"It will be as I said. How dare you question me? Do you reprove your King? Take warning from the shepherd's fate."

"Do you threaten a companion's life?" the war-leader flung back, his lips white with rage. "Know, Rhitta, you have a warrior to deal with, not a weak old man. You, sire, take warning yourself."

At this, Rhitta struck the war-leader across the face and cried:

"Be gone! Do you covet more land? For your insolence, your own lands are forfeit. I banish you from court and castle, and from all my realm."

Seeing Rhitta's fury, neither the councilors nor any of the nobles dared gainsay the King. So the war-leader was sent away in disgrace and his place given to another.

That night in his bed chamber, when he laid aside the sword, Rhitta saw the stain had not only darkened but spread until it covered still more of the scabbard. Again he tried to wipe it away, but the stubborn stain remained and grew larger. Alarmed, he gave the weapon to his master swordsmiths, but even they could not scour it clean.

Now, at this same time, many nobles, witnesses to the war-leader's disgrace, began muttering among themselves. The King's injustice rankled them, and they feared his wrath might fall heavily upon them, too, and strip them of their own lands and honors. So they swore to rise against the King and overthrow him.

But Rhitta had word of their plan, and even as they gathered to do battle, Rhitta and his war band rode out and set upon them, taking them by surprise.

As it happened, the place of battle was none other than the field of Amrys, the shepherd. And Rhitta, leading his warriors, suddenly cried out in horror. There, before his eyes, stood the shepherd, bloody with wounds, holding out the lamb to him.

The King's warriors, seeing nothing, took Rhitta's outburst as a battle cry. They galloped to a fierce charge, slew most of those who stood against them, and put the rest to flight.

Rhitta, however, had reined his horse and turned from the

fray. With all speed, he rode back to his castle and lay trembling in his chamber, certain the shepherd had meant to work some evil upon him.

When his warriors brought him word of the victory and asked if he had been wounded and therefore had not led the onslaught, Rhitta dared not speak of what he had seen. Instead, he told them he had been stricken with a sudden fever and sickness. But he could not keep the shepherd from his thoughts.

"He deserved his fate," Rhitta repeated to himself. "As do all who have risen against me. Let their lands, too, be forfeit, and their goods and gold be added to the royal treasure."

But now the stain spread farther and blotted nearly all the scabbard. Again Rhitta ordered his swordsmiths to find a means of scouring it. They could not.

"The metal is flawed," Rhitta cried. "The sword is ill-made."

At the same time, uneasiness filled his mind. Now he believed the sight of Amrys had been an omen and a warning of more treachery. And so he called his councilors, war-leader, and captains of his war bands, saying:

"All our enemies are not yet overcome, and the danger to the kingdom is even greater. The kinsmen of those traitors will surely seek vengeance. It may be they plot against me even now. It may be they bide their time, waiting for a day when they shall rise and strike me unawares. Better that I crush them before they can rally in strength and set upon me."

So Rhitta commanded his war bands to arm and at dawn be ready to seek out the traitors' kindred and to slay them.

That night, however, Rhitta turned and tossed on his couch, and long before dawn he woke at the sound of a voice murmuring in his chamber. He started up, sweating in terror, to see the shepherd, holding the lamb in his arms, standing at the foot of the couch. And Amrys spoke and said:

"Remember the broken gate, sire. Remember the lost sheep. The path you follow leads you, too, astray. Mourn the dead by pitying the living."

The shepherd would have spoken further, but Rhitta, unheeding, sprang up with a great cry, seized Dyrnwyn, and made to snatch the blade from its sheath. But the scabbard held the blade with jaws of iron. In fear and rage, Rhitta clawed at the weapon and tore at it until his fingers were bloodied. He could not draw the sword.

When his guards ran to him with torches, he ordered them away, saying only that he had had a bad dream. But in the morning, while his warriors stood by their horses, awaiting him to mount and ride at the head of the battle host, Rhitta summoned his war-leader and told him:

"I have thought on this, and see it is not fitting for a King to show concern in such a matter. Were I myself to lead the host, there would be those to say I judged the danger greater than it is, or even that I had no trust in my officers. Therefore, go and do my bidding as it seems best to you, in any way you choose."

Then Rhitta withdrew to his chamber, never daring to tell the true reason behind his words.

It is written on the scabbard, thought Rhitta, *Draw Dyrnwyn, only thou of noble worth*. Since the blade will not come freely to my hand, my warriors may believe their King is unworthy to rule.

The more he stared at the inscription, the more the words of it mocked him. With a curse, Rhitta seized a dagger and tried to scratch away the graven message. Though he marred some of the letters, the engraving remained and stood out all the brighter against the scabbard. Then Rhitta flung aside the dagger. Clutching the sword, he crouched trembling in a corner of his chamber, his eyes glittering feverishly, his glance never at rest.

Soon his war-leader came to him and said:

"Sire, the kinsmen of our enemies are slain, and all their families, their wives and mothers, their children, and any who might claim blood kinship with them."

Rhitta nodded vaguely, as if he had not heard, and murmured:

"You have done well."

Afterward, Rhitta looked again at Dyrnwyn. It had turned altogether black.

That night, although he slept behind barred and bolted doors, he woke to the sound of weeping and once more saw the shepherd, who turned an anguished face upon him and called out:

"Sire, find yourself before you lose yourself."

Rhitta stopped his ears against these words, but even the coming of day did not dissolve his nightmare, and the empty chamber echoed the shepherd's weeping.

"Another omen," cried Rhitta. "Another warning that all my enemies are not yet slain. All must be found and killed, or I shall lose my kingdom."

So he commanded his war bands to hunt down any who had ever befriended the kinsmen of his enemies; any who spoke in favor of them; and any who did not praise the worthiness of his kingship.

Even this brought him no peace. While Rhitta stayed in his chamber, his warriors roved the kingdom unchecked, putting many to the sword, with or without cause, having more thought now to seizing treasure than finding treachery. However, instead of striking terror in the hearts of Rhitta's foes, such deeds only enraged them and gave them the courage of despair. Where before there had been few, now arose many who joined to fight against the King. And Rhitta's nightmares, instead of easing, grew more terrible. He feared to stay alone in his chamber and feared to leave it, sure some hand would strike him down even amid his bodyguard.

So Rhitta commanded new chambers be made for him deep underground, with heavy doors and thick walls. At the same time he ordered his henchmen to stand circling his couch with drawn swords and keep watch over him.

Now, each night, Rhitta slept in a different chamber. Not even his councilors could be certain where to find him. Next he commanded other rooms to be built, with hallways, tunnels, and galleries, winding and crossing, twisting and turning, in a pattern he alone could fathom. Thus the stronghold became known as Spiral Castle.

Even then Rhitta was unsatisfied. He commanded his builders to dig still deeper, until they could go no farther. There they hewed a chamber out of living rock, in which he heaped great stores of provisions, treasures of gold and goods, coffers of jewels, robes of rich fur, and stacks of finely wrought weapons. He raised a high couch where he lay with the black sword at his hand. At last Rhitta was content. No enemy could find him, no battle host breach the walls. Even so, he ordered his warriors to stand about him with naked blades.

That night he went easily to sleep. But soon, as before, anguished murmuring aroused him. There stood the shepherd, his wounds running red, staining the fleece of the lamb he carried.

The warriors, sure no danger was possible, had fallen asleep on the floor. Rhitta would have cried an alarm, but his voice turned to stone in his throat as Amrys drew closer.

"Wretched King," came the shepherd's sorrowing voice. "Alas, you would not heed me. You slew me once for a broken gate; but you have slain yourself a hundred times over. King, I pity you as I would pity any suffering creature."

The shepherd reached out a hand as if he would touch Rhitta's brow.

Seeing this, fearing that Amrys meant to strike him, Rhitta found his voice again and shrieked in terror. At the same time, bending all his might, straining every sinew in a final effort, he clutched the hilt of Dyrnwyn and strove to rip it from the scabbard. He shouted in triumph as the blade came free.

But he had unsheathed only a hand's-breadth of the blade when tongues of white flame burst crackling from the hilt and all the length of the scabbard. Where before he had been unable to draw the weapon, now he could not unclench his fists and cast the blazing sword away.

Like a lightning bolt, the flame filled the chamber in an instant, striking down even the guards who staggered to their feet. Then, as suddenly as it had risen, the flame was quenched. Still gripping the blackened sword in his lifeless hands, King Rhitta fell back on his couch. And all was silent.

Because no one could find a way through the tunnels and galleries, Rhitta lay as he had fallen. In time, having no word of him, his councilors and courtiers at last knew him to be dead.

And only the shepherd Amrys ever grieved for him.

# The Smith,
# The Weaver,
## and
# The Harper

There was a time in Prydain when craftsmen were so skillful their very tools held the secrets of their crafts. Of these, the hammer of Iscovan the Smith could work any metal into whatever shape its owner wished. The shuttle of Follin the Weaver could weave quicker than the eye could see, with never a knot or a tangle. The harp of Menwy the Bard sounded airs of such beauty it lifted the hearts of all who heard it.

But Arawn, Lord of Death, coveted these things and set out to gain them for himself, to lock them deep in his treasure-house, so no man might ever have use of them.

And so it was that one day, working at his anvil, Iscovan saw a tall man standing in his doorway. The stranger was arrayed as a war-leader, sword at side, shield over shoulder; he wore a coat of mail whose links were so cleverly wrought and burnished it seemed smooth as satin and glittering as gold.

"Blacksmith," said the tall man, "the rowel of my spur is broken. Can you mend it?"

"There's no metal in all this world I can't mend, or shape, or temper," Iscovan answered. "A broken spur? A trifle! Here, put it on my anvil. With this hammer of mine I'll have it done in three strokes."

"You have a fair hammer," the warrior said, "but I doubt it can work metal such as this."

"Think you so?" cried Iscovan, stung by these words. "Well, now, see for yourself."

So saying, he laid the spur on his anvil, picked up his hammer, and began pounding away with all the strength of his burly arms.

At last, out of breath, his brow smudged and streaming, he stopped and frowned at the spur. It showed not the least mark from his battering.

Iscovan pumped the bellows of his forge, picked up the spur with his tongs, and thrust it into his furnace. There, heating it white-hot, once again he set it on his anvil, and hammered as hard as he was able, to no avail.

"Trouble yourself no more," the stranger told the puzzled blacksmith. "In my country, armorers shape metal harder than any you know. If you would do likewise, you must use a hammer like theirs."

With that, he reached into a leather sack hanging from his belt and took out a little golden hammer, which he handed to the smith.

"That toy?" Iscovan burst out. "Make sport of me and you'll have more than a broken spur to mend!"

"Try it, nevertheless," replied the stranger.

Laughing scornfully, the smith gripped the hammer and struck with all his force, sure the implement would break in his hand. Instead, sparks shot up, there came a roar of thunder, and his anvil split nearly in two. However, after that single blow, the spur was good as new.

Iscovan's jaw dropped and he stared at the tall man, who said:

"My thanks to you, blacksmith. Now let me take my hammer and go my way."

"Wait," said Iscovan, clutching the tool. "Tell me first how I might get a hammer like yours."

"In my realm, these are treasured highly," replied the stranger. "You have only seen the smallest part of its worth. With such a hammer a smith can forge weapons that lose neither point nor edge, shields that never split, coats of mail no sword can pierce. Thus arrayed, even a handful of warriors could master a kingdom."

"Tell me nothing of arms and armor," Iscovan replied. "I'm no swordsmith; my skill is with plow-irons, rakes, and hoes. But, one way or another, I must have that hammer."

Now Iscovan had always been a peaceful man; but even as he spoke these words, his head began spinning with secret thoughts. The stranger's voice seemed to fan embers in his mind until they glowed hotter than his forge. And Iscovan said to himself, "If this man speaks the truth, and no sword or spear can harm them, indeed a handful of warriors could master a kingdom, for who could stand against them? But the smith who had the secret—he would be master of all! And why not I instead of another?"

The stranger, who meantime had been watching Iscovan narrowly, said:

"Blacksmith, you have done me a favor and by rights I owe a favor to you. So, I shall give you this hammer. But for the sake of a fair bargain, give me yours in its place."

Iscovan hesitated, picking up his old hammer and looking fondly at it. The handle was worn smooth by long use, the iron head was nicked and dented; yet this hammer knew its craft as deeply as Iscovan himself, for it had taken to itself the skill of all smiths. It had well served Iscovan and brought him the honor of his workmanship. Nevertheless, considering what new power lay within his grasp, Iscovan nodded and said:

"Done. So be it."

The stranger took Iscovan's iron hammer, leaving the gold one in the hands of the smith, and without another word strode from the forge.

No sooner had the stranger gone than Iscovan, with a triumphant cry, raised the hammer and gave his anvil a ringing blow. But even as he did, the hammer crumbled in his hand. The bright gold had turned to lead.

Bewildered, Iscovan stared at the useless tool, then ran from the forge, shouting for his own hammer back again. Of the stranger, however, there was no trace.

And from that time on, Iscovan drudged at his forge, never to find a hammer the equal of the one he had bartered away.

On another day, Follin the Weaver was busy at his loom when a short, thickset man, ruddy-cheeked and quick-eyed, came into his weaving shed. Follin stopped plying his shuttle, which had been darting back and forth among the threads like a fish in water.

"Good greeting to you," said the stranger, clad in garments finer than any the weaver had ever seen. His heavy cloak was of cloth of gold, embroidered in curious patterns. "My cloak is worn and shabby. Will you weave another for me?"

"I don't know where you're from," returned Follin, dazzled at the traveler's apparel, "but surely it's a rich realm if you call that handsome cloak shabby."

"It serves well enough to wear on a journey, to be stained and spattered," returned the traveler. "But in my country this is no better than a castoff. Even a beggar would scorn it."

Follin, meanwhile, had climbed down from his bench at the loom. He could not take his eyes from the stranger's cloak, and when he ventured to rub the hem between his thumb and fingers, he grew still more amazed. The cloth, although purest gold, was lighter than thistledown and softer than lamb's wool.

"I can weave nothing like this," Follin stammered. "I have no thread to match it, and the work is beyond even my skill."

"It would be a simple matter," said the traveler, "if you had the means." He reached into a leather sack he carried at his belt. "Here, try this shuttle instead of yours."

Doubtfully, Follin took the shuttle, which looked as if it had never been used, while his own was worn and polished and comfortable to his hand. Nevertheless, at the stranger's bidding, Follin threw the shuttle across the threads already on his loom.

That same instant, the shuttle began flying back and forth even faster than his old one. In moments, before the weaver's eyes, shimmering cloth of gold appeared and grew so quickly the loom soon held enough for a cloak.

"Weaver, my thanks to you," said the stranger, gesturing for Follin to take the new cloth off the loom. "What reward shall you ask?"

Follin was too dumbfounded to do more than wag his head and gape at the work of the wondrous shuttle. And so the traveler continued:

"You have done me a favor. Now I shall do one for you. Keep the shuttle. Use it as it may best profit you."

"What?" cried Follin, scarcely believing his ears. "You mean to give me such a treasure?"

"Treasure it may be to you," replied the stranger, "not to me. In my country, such implements are commonplace. Nevertheless," he went on, "for the sake of a fair bargain, give me your shuttle in trade and you shall have this one."

Now Follin had never been a greedy man. But the traveler's words were like thin fingers plucking at the warp and weft of his thoughts. He had used his old shuttle all his life, and knew it to be filled with the wisdom and pride of his workmanship. Even so, he told himself, no man in his wits could turn down such an exchange. Instead of cloth, he could weave all the gold he wanted. And so he said:

"Done. So be it."

He handed his old shuttle to the traveler, who popped it into the leather sack and, without another word, left the weaving shed.

No sooner had the stranger gone out the door than Follin, trembling in excitement, leaped onto his bench and set about weaving as fast as he could. He laughed with glee and his eyes glittered at the treasure that would be his.

"I'll weave myself a fortune!" he cried. "And when I've spent that, I'll weave myself another! And another! I'll be the richest man in all the land. I'll dine from gold plates, I'll drink from gold cups!"

Suddenly the flying shuttle stopped, split asunder, and fell in pieces to the ground. On the loom the gleaming threads turned, in that instant, to cobwebs and tore apart in shreds before Follin's eyes.

Distraught at the cheat, bewailing the loss of his shuttle, Follin ran from the weaving shed. But the traveler had gone.

And from that time on, Follin drudged at his loom, never to find a shuttle the equal of the one he had bartered away.

On another day, Menwy the Bard was sitting under a tree, tuning his harp, when a lean-faced man, cloaked in gray and mounted on a pale horse, reined up and called to him:

"Harper, my instrument lacks a string. Can you spare me one of yours?"

Menwy noticed the rider carried at his saddle bow a golden harp, the fairest he had ever seen. He got to his feet and strode up to the horseman to admire the instrument more closely.

"Alas, friend," said Menwy, "I have no strings to match yours. Mine are of the common kind, but yours are spun of gold and silver. If it plays as nobly as it looks, you should be proud of it."

"In my country," said the rider, "this would be deemed the meanest of instruments. But since it seems to please you, so you shall have it. For the sake of a fair bargain, though, give me yours in exchange."

"Now what a marvelous place the world is!" Menwy answered lightly. "Here's a fellow who rides out of nowhere, and asks nothing better than to do me a favor. And would I be so ungrateful as to turn it down? Come, friend, before there's any talk of trading this and that, let's hear a tune from that handsome harp of yours."

At this, the rider stiffened and raised a hand as if the bard had threatened him; but, recovering himself, he replied:

"Prove the instrument for yourself, harper. Take it in your hands, listen to its voice."

Menwy shook his head. "No need, friend. For I can tell you now, even though yours sang like a nightingale, I'd rather keep my own. I know its ways, and it knows mine."

The rider's eyes flickered for an instant. Then he replied:

"Harper, your fame has spread even as far as my realm. Scorn my gift as you will. But come with me and I swear you shall serve a king more powerful than any in Prydain. His bard you shall be, and you shall have a seat of honor by his throne."

"How could that be?" asked Menwy, smiling. "Already I serve a ruler greater than yours, for I serve my music."

Now Menwy was a poet and used to seeing around the edge of

things. All this while, he had been watching the gray-cloaked horseman; and now as he looked closer, the rider and the golden harp seemed to change before his eyes. The frame of the instrument, which had appeared so fair, he saw to be wrought of dry bones, and the strings were serpents poised to strike.

Though Menwy was as brave as any man, the sight of the rider's true face behind its mask of flesh froze the harper's blood. Nevertheless, he did not turn away, nor did his glance waver as he replied:

"I see you for what you are, Lord of Death. And I fear you, as all men do. For all that, you are a weak and pitiful king. You can destroy, but never build. You are less than the humblest creature, the frailest blade of grass. For these live, and every moment of their lives is a triumph over you. Your kingdom is dust; only the silent ending of things, never the beginning."

At that, Menwy took his harp and began to play a joyful melody. Hearing it, the horseman's face tightened in rage; he drew his sword from its sheath and with all his might he struck at the bard.

But the blow missed its mark and instead struck the harp, shattering it to bits. Menwy, however, flung aside the pieces, threw back his head, and laughed in defiance, calling out:

"You fail, Death-Lord! You destroy the instrument, but not its music. With all your power you have gained only a broken shell."

In that moment, when the harp had been silenced, arose the songs of birds, the chiming of brooks, the humming of wind through grass and leaves; and all these voices took up the strands of melody, more beautiful than before.

And the Lord of Death fled in terror of life.

# Coll and His White Pig

This is the brave tale of Coll and his white pig, and what befell them in the faraway Land of Prydain.

And this is the beginning of it.

Coll, in his younger days, had been a dauntless warrior. Now, grown a little stout around the middle, and much lacking in hair on the crown of his head, he had taken to farming.

"I have had my fill of wild adventuring, whatever," said Coll.

So he made a plow-iron out of his sword and beanpoles from his old spears; and sparrows nested in his leather fighting cap. Not even Dallben, the most powerful enchanter in Prydain, had greater skill in plowing, planting, or harvesting than Coll. No man was as good-natured with a garden, as tender-hearted with a tree, or as agreeable with animals. He loved his vegetable plot, his apple orchard, and, above all, his white pig, Hen Wen.

One night, Coll had gone to bed worried over his turnips, which were coming up sickly that year; and he tossed and turned, wondering what to do about them. He was barely asleep when a thunder of hoofbeats aroused him. Next, he heard Hen Wen squealing at the top of her voice. Coll leaped up, pulled on his boots, flung a cloak around him, and was out the cottage door in a moment.

He glimpsed a band of horsemen galloping off into the forest. One rider had flung Hen Wen, shrieking and struggling, over his saddlebow. Shouting, Coll raced after them. For a time, he ran as fast as he could in the darkness, following the crashing of the steeds through the underbrush. But the riders outdistanced him and, at last, in the dawn mist, Coll dropped to the ground, out of breath, deeply distressed, having not the first notion of who had made off with his pig nor where they had taken her.

To restore his strength, Coll looked for roots and berries. Breakfast was a meal he always relished, but he found only a handful of hazelnuts. He had just finished munching them and was pondering what next to do, when he heard pitiful cries from a fallen tree nearby. An owlet was trapped in the tree trunk. The two owls fluttered desperately around it, but their efforts availed them nothing. Carefully, Coll freed the owlet and put it back in the nest, where the mother flew to join it.

The second owl perched on a limb above Coll's head. "My name is Ash-Wing," said the owl. "My wife and I thank you for your kindness."

"You are welcome to my help," said Coll, taken aback, "but I never thought owls could speak."

"Eggshells!" retorted Ash-Wing. "All creatures can speak. Until now, it is you who have not understood."

"How then?" said Coll, puzzled. "I have done nothing but munch a few hazelnuts, and meager fare they were."

"Surprising how little you humans know of such matters," replied the owl. "Those were Hazelnuts of Wisdom. Only one tree in Prydain bears them. Luckily, you found it."

"Alas," said Coll, "I still have not wisdom enough to learn who stole my pig, or why."

"As to who," said Ash-Wing, "it was King Arawn of Annuvin,

Lord of the Land of Death. As to why, it is because Hen Wen is no ordinary pig. She knows many deep secrets. Arawn has stolen her to find them out, and use them in his evil scheme to conquer all Prydain."

Coll turned pale and his blood ran cold. The Lord of the Land of Death was the enemy most dreaded throughout Prydain. "For the sake of Hen Wen, I would brave Arawn himself," said Coll. "But even if I could find my way, his guards would discover me before I set one foot within Annuvin." Coll put his head in his hands. "My pig is lost, and Prydain is doomed."

"Pinfeathers!" said Ash-Wing. "We owls know all the forest paths, and I will guide you to Annuvin. Under cover of darkness, you can slip past the guards. I will show you how, for I see better at midnight than other creatures see at noon. By the way, how many hazelnuts did you eat?"

When Coll replied that he did not know, Ash-Wing blinked at him. "Who but a human would eat them without counting! Let me tell you this: each nut is a day given you to understand the speech of birds and animals. When that power is gone, I can help no longer."

Hurriedly, Coll set out again with Ash-Wing on his shoulder. Though Coll's fear for his pig had grown greater, his heart also turned to his farm. "The worms will have their joy of my cabbages," said Coll to himself. "And blight on my beans. And scale on my apple trees. And my poor turnips—surely this is the end of them, whatever."

He had journeyed less than a day, following the owl's guidance, when a thrashing noise broke into his thoughts. A tall stag had caught his antlers in a thornbush, and the more the creature struggled, the more he was entangled. Ash-Wing fluttered overhead while Coll, heedless of his torn garments and the deep scratches on his face and hands, ripped away the sharp thorns.

The stag leaped free, then bowed his head courteously to Coll. "My name is Oak-Horn," said the stag, "and I owe you my life. The Huntsmen of King Arawn ride abroad! Had they found me—my antlers tremble at the thought!"

"Tarry no longer," Ash-Wing cried to Coll. "Not only may the Huntsmen come upon us. The power of the hazelnuts may leave you before we reach Annuvin."

"Annuvin?" gasped Oak-Horn. "The very name makes my antlers wilt!"

When Coll told of his quest, the stag shuddered and rolled his eyes fearfully. "To be truthful," said Oak-Horn, "we stags are not—well, we are not the boldest folk in the forest. But we are the swiftest. If speed can help you, I will do my best."

Oak-Horn bore Coll on his back and Ash-Wing perched atop the stag's antlers. As they quickly journeyed on, Coll yearned more and more for his comfortable chair by his warm fireside.

"And by this time," sighed Coll, "the beetles will be hard at work in my garden; that is, if they can find it under the weeds. As for my unhappy turnips—best not even think of them."

Suddenly, Oak-Horn reared up. A bird greater than the greatest eagle beat its wings and clawed savagely at a cleft rock. A tiny mole was cornered there, unable to flee or dig to safety. Coll sprang from Oak-Horn's back, snatched up a branch, and laid about him so furiously that the huge bird took flight.

"A gwythaint!" cried Oak-Horn, in such alarm that his antlers quivered. "One of King Arawn's messengers! It will carry news of us to the Land of Death. Ah, Coll, your quest is ruined. Ruined for a mere mole!"

"Mere mole indeed!" squealed the little creature. "I am Star-Nose, Chief Mole of Prydain. In all our councils and clans, our fellowships and families, the name of Coll will be honored."

The mole scurried away. Ash-Wing urged all possible haste, and they set off once more. While the owl grumbled bitterly at the pridefulness of moles, and the stag shivered with fright at every step, Coll was silent and heavy-hearted. He feared his gift of understanding might vanish at any moment. Even if it did not, the gwythaint would surely raise the alarm in Annuvin. "Yet I could do no less than help the unlucky mole," said Coll to himself, "and glad enough I was to do so. Nevertheless, honor to my name is no help to my pig and cold comfort to my turnips."

For some days they journeyed, Ash-Wing leading the way, Oak-Horn bearing Coll across rivers and along cruel mountain trails. At last, by night, they drew near the Dark Gate of Annuvin. Here, the owl spied out a hidden passage and the stag, despite quaking heart and quivering antlers, carried Coll down the twisting, treacherous path. Silent as shadows, they stole unseen into the depths of Arawn's realm.

Ash-Wing had flown ahead to find where Hen Wen had been taken. "Woeful news!" hooted the owl, returning. "She is prisoned in a deep pit, guarded by Huntsmen and fierce gwythaints. She is so terrified she cannot speak. Thus, Arawn has learned none of her secrets. But now he means to slay her."

"He shall slay me first!" cried Coll, leaping from the stag's back. "I will fight for my pig to the last!"

"Stay!" warned Ash-Wing. "First let me see what I may do."

Ash-Wing sped into the air. Catching sight of the owl, the gwythaints screamed with bloodlust and swooped to follow him.

Taking courage from Ash-Wing's example, Oak-Horn bounded forward. The Huntsmen shouted, drew their swords, and left the pit to pursue the stag.

Coll's way now lay clear. He raced ahead and flung himself into the unguarded pit, where Hen Wen squealed joyfully to see him. Desperately, Coll sought an escape for them. There was none. The pit was too deep; the walls were too sheer. Coll heard the clashing weapons of the returning Huntsmen, the beating wings of the gwythaints. All hope lost, Coll stood over his pig, vowing to sell his life dearly. Spears whistled down, arrows hissed, and Coll knew the end had come.

Suddenly, at his feet the pit opened. There stood Star-Nose, and behind him, moles in their dozens and hundreds and thousands.

"Quickly!" squeaked Star-Nose. "All our councils and clans, our fellowships and families have labored for you. Our tunnel will lead you to safety!"

Coll seized Hen Wen, thrust her into the mouth of the tunnel, and scrambled after. Behind him, Star-Nose and the others walled up the opening against the Huntsmen. At every turn, from every side, the moles cheered Coll and his white pig all along the way.

Far from Annuvin, the tunnel ended and they clambered above ground. Ash-Wing and Oak-Horn, having escaped unharmed, joined them again and began the journey back to Coll's farm. When at last they arrived at the edge of the woods, the owl and the stag halted.

"Farewell, Coll," said Ash-Wing. "If you ever need eyes to see in the darkness, call on me."

"Farewell, Coll," said Oak-Horn. "My heart is still in my mouth, but if you ever need a swift foot, call on me."

"And if you ever need work well done," piped up Star-Nose, who had been lying in a fold of Coll's cloak this while, "do not forget us."

"Farewell," said Coll. "I shall forget none of you."

He turned from the forest. The voices of his friends faded behind him and he knew, sadly, that his power to understand their speech had ended. Hen Wen, her stubby trotters flying, ran beside him, as he hastened to his farm.

Amazed, Coll stopped short. Not a weed did he see; nor, at a quick glance, any sign of worms in the cabbages, blight on the beans, or scale on the apple trees. Yet he was more alarmed than pleased, because smoke was curling out of the cottage chimney.

"Alas," cried Coll, dismayed, "I have found my pig and lost my farm."

He stepped past the door. A fire crackled merrily in the hearth, and in Coll's chair sat a gray-bearded stranger, so ancient that his hands seemed brittle as autumn leaves, his face lined like frost tracings on an ice-bound river. Though Coll was a bold man, he drew back a little fearfully before the flame of authority in the stranger's pale eyes.

"A good greeting to you, Coll," said the aged man, not troubling to get up. "If I had reached here sooner, I might have spared you a harsh journey. I sensed Hen Wen's danger and set out to warn you. I arrived a little late; but no matter. You have done well enough on your own. And I have whiled away the time tending your garden. You know me not," he added, seeing Coll's bewilderment, "but I know you, and the worth of your pig. I am Dallben."

Few in Prydain had looked face to face upon this mighty

enchanter, and Coll bowed most humbly. For her part, Hen Wen sat on her haunches and grinned happily.

"No doing of mine," replied Coll, and he told what had befallen him along the way.

"Tut," said Dallben. "Look at the root of things, and see that what truly counts is not a strong arm but a kind heart; not a fist that smites but a hand that helps."

The enchanter then pointed to a great leather-bound book on the table. "This is *The Book of Three*, and in it is set down all that will happen in the days to come. These things are hidden from you now, but I grant you the gift of knowing one of them. Which shall it be?"

Coll's bald head turned pink and he pulled nervously at his ear, for he was a modest man and unused to such favors.

"Now then," he answered, thinking hard, "I already know that spring will surely follow winter; and just as surely there will be sunlight and rain, good days and bad. And if I am to have any more such adventures—why, I would rather not know about them ahead of time. It is a great gift you offer me; but, thank you all the same, I have no need of it."

"Think well," said Dallben. "This chance will not be given to you again."

"Wait!" cried Coll. "Yes, there is one matter I would know above all. Tell me, then, tell me, for it has been on my mind these many days: how shall my turnips fare this year?"

Dallben smiled. "To answer that, I need not open *The Book of Three*," he replied. "They will thrive."

It was true, even as Dallben had said. Coll's turnips had never been bigger or tastier. Dallben himself agreed to remain at the farm, which greatly pleased Coll—not only for the honor of it, but for the safety of Hen Wen. And all prospered.

"No doubt about it," said Coll to Hen Wen. "It is better to be raising things up than smiting things down. And quieter, into the bargain."

Such is the tale of Coll and the rescuing of Hen Wen, with the help of the owl, Ash-Wing, the stag, Oak-Horn, and the digging and delving of the moles.

And such is the end of it.

# The Truthful Harp

This is the tale of King Fflewddur Fflam and his truthful harp, as the bards tell it in the Land of Prydain.

And this is the beginning of it.

Fflewddur Fflam ruled a kingdom so small he could almost stride across it between midday and high noon. The fields and pastures grew so near his castle that sheep and cows ambled up to gaze into his bed-chamber; and the cottagers' children played in his Great Hall, knowing he would sooner join their games than order them away.

"My crown's a grievous burden!" Fflewddur cried. "That is, it would be if I ever wore it. But a Fflam is dutiful! My subjects need me to rule this vast kingdom with a firm hand and a watchful eye!"

Nevertheless, one secret wish lay closest to his heart. He yearned to adventure as a wandering bard.

"A Fflam is eager!" he declared. "I'll be as great a bard as I am a king!"

So he puzzled over tomes of ancient lore, striving to gain the wisdom every true bard must have. And he strained and struggled with his harp until his fingers blistered.

"A Fflam is clever!" he exclaimed. "I'll soon have the knack of it, and play my harp as well as I rule my kingdom!"

At last he fancied himself ready to stand before the High Council of Bards and ask to be ranked among their number.

"A Fflam goes forth!" cried Fflewddur. "Gird on my sword! Saddle my charger! But have a care, she's wild and mettlesome."

All his subjects who could spare the time gathered to cheer him on, to wave farewell, and to wish him good speed.

"It saddens them to see me go," Fflewddur sighed. "But a Fflam is faithful! Even as a famous bard, I'll do my kingly duty as carefully as ever."

And so he journeyed to golden-towered Caer Dathyl and eagerly hastened to the Council Chamber.

"A Fflam is quick-witted!" he cried confidently. "Prove me as you please! I've got every morsel of learning on the tip of my tongue, and every harp tune at my fingers' ends!"

However, when the Council and the Chief Bard questioned him deeply, all that Fflewddur had learned flew out of his head like a flock of sparrows. He gave the right answers to the wrong questions, the wrong answers to the right questions; and worst of all, when he fumbled to strike a tune on his harp it slipped from his grasp and shattered in a thousand splinters on the flagstones. Then Fflewddur bowed his head and stared wretchedly at his boots, knowing he had failed.

"Alas, you are not ready to be one of us," the Chief Bard regretfully told him. But then, with all his poet's wisdom and compassion, the Chief Bard pitied the hapless king, and spoke apart with a servant, desiring him to bring a certain harp which he put in Fflewddur's hands.

"You still have much to learn," said the Chief Bard. "Perhaps this may help you."

Seeing the harp, Fflewddur's dismay vanished in that instant, and his face beamed with delight. The beautiful instrument seemed to play of itself. He needed only touch his fingers to the strings and melodies poured forth in a golden tide.

"Good riddance to my old pot!" Fflewddur cried. "Here's a harp that shows my true skill. A Fflam is grateful!"

The Chief Bard smiled within himself. "May you ever be as grateful as you are now. Come back when it pleases you to tell us how you have fared."

High-hearted, Fflewddur set out from Caer Dathyl. His new harp gladdened him as much as if he were in fact a bard, and he rode along playing merrily and singing at the top of his voice.

Nearing a river he came upon an old man painfully gathering twigs for a fire. Winter had hardly ended, and a chill wind still bit sharply, and the old man's threadbare garments gave no comfort against the cold. He shivered in the gale, his lips were bitter blue, and his fingers were so numb he could scarcely pick up his twigs.

"A good greeting, friend," called Fflewddur. "Brisk weather may be good for the blood, but it seems to me you're ill-garbed for a day like this."

"No warmer clothing do I have," replied the old man. "Would that I did, for I'm frozen to the marrow of my bones."

"Then take my cloak," urged Fflewddur, doffing his garment and wrapping it about the old man's shoulders.

"My thanks to you," said the old man, wistfully fondling the cloak. "But I cannot take what you yourself need."

"Need?" exclaimed Fflewddur. "Not at all," he added, though his own lips had begun turning blue and his nose felt as if it had grown icicles. "Take it and welcome. For the truth of the matter is, I find the day uncomfortably hot!"

No sooner had he spoken these words than the harp shuddered as if it were alive, bent like an overdrawn bow, and a string snapped in two with a loud twang.

"Drat that string!" muttered Fflewddur. "The weather's got into it somehow."

Knotting up the string, he set out on his way again, shivering, shaking, and playing for all he was worth to keep himself warm.

He wandered on, following the swiftly flowing river. Suddenly he heard a child's voice crying in distress and terror. Clapping heels to his horse's flank he galloped down the riverbank. A small girl had tumbled into the water and the hapless child struggled vainly against the current already sweeping her away.

Fflewddur leaped from his mount and plunged with a great splash into the river, flailing his arms, thrashing his legs, striving with all his might to reach the drowning child.

"This would be an easy task," he gasped, "if only I could swim!"

Nonetheless, he pressed on, choking and sputtering, until he caught up the child. Keeping afloat as best he could, he turned shoreward; at last his long shanks found footing on the riverbed, and he bore the girl safely to dry land.

Comforting her all the while, though water streamed from his nose, ears, and mouth, he made his way to the cottage from which she had strayed. There, the husbandman and his wife joyously threw their arms about their daughter and the bedraggled Fflewddur as well.

"Poor folk we are," cried the farm wife. "What reward can we give? All we have is yours, and small payment for saving our greatest treasure."

"Don't give it a thought," Fflewddur exclaimed, his face lighting up as he warmed to his tale. "Why, to begin with, it was in my mind to have a dip in the river. As for the rest—a trifle! A Fflam swims like a fish! With only a few powerful strokes—"

The harp twitched violently and a pair of strings gave way with an earsplitting crack.

"Drat and blast!" muttered Fflewddur. "What ails these beastly strings? The dampness, I'll be bound."

Taking his leave of the family, for some days he wandered happily to his heart's content, finding himself at last before the stronghold of a noble lord. To the guards at the gate, Fflewddur called out that a bard had come with music and merriment, whereupon they welcomed him and led him to the lord's Great Hall.

No sooner had Fflewddur begun to play than the lord leaped angrily from his throne.

"Have done!" he burst out. "You yelp like a cur with its tail trodden, and your harp rattles worse than a kettle of stones! Away with you!"

Before Fflewddur could collect his wits, the lord snatched up a cudgel, collared the harper, and began drubbing him with all his strength.

"Ai! Ow! Have a care!" cried Fflewddur, struggling vainly to escape the blows and shield his harp at the same time. "A king am I! Of the mightiest realm in Prydain! You'll rue this day when you see my battle host at your gates! A thousand warriors! Spearmen! Bowmen! A Fflam at their head!"

While the harp strings broke right and left, the lord seized Fflewddur by the scruff of the neck and flung him out the gate, where he landed headlong in the mire.

"A Fflam humiliated!" Fflewddur cried, painfully climbing to his feet. "Affronted! Beaten like a knave!" He rubbed his aching shoulders. "Yes, well, it's clear," he sighed. "Some people have no ear for music."

His bones too sore for the saddle, he made the rest of his way afoot, with his horse jogging after him. He had trudged a little distance when the selfsame lord and his train of servants galloped by.

"What, are you still in my domain?" shouted the lord. "Begone, you spindle-shanked scarecrow! If once again I see that long nose of yours, you'll have a drubbing better than the first!"

Fflewddur held his tongue as the horsemen rode past, fearing more for his harp than his skin. "Stone-eared clot!" he grumbled under his breath. "A Fflam is forgiving, but this is more than any man can bear." And he consoled himself with delicious dreams of how he would even the score—should he ever have a host of warriors at his command.

Suddenly he realized the clash of arms and noise of battle came not from his imaginings but from a short way down the road. A band of robbers, lying in ambush, had set upon the riders. The servants had fled bawling in terror and the lord himself was hard pressed and sorely in danger of losing his head as well as his purse.

Snatching out his sword and shouting his battle cry, "A Fflam! A Fflam!" Fflewddur rushed into the fray, and laid about him so fiercely and ferociously the robbers turned and fled as if a whole army of long-legged madmen were at their heels.

Shamefaced, the lord knelt humbly before him, saying: "Alas, I gave you a cudgel to your back, but you gave me a bold sword at my side."

"Ah—yes, well, for the matter of that," replied Fflewddur, a little tartly now the danger was past, "the truth is, a Fflam is hotblooded! I'd been itching for a good fight all this day. But had I known it was you," he added, "believe me, I'd have kept on my way—Oh, not again! Drat and blast the wretched things!" He moaned as three harp strings broke one after the other, and the instrument jangled as if it would fall to bits.

More than ever dismayed at the state of his harp strings, Fflewddur left the lord's domain and turned back toward Caer Dathyl, journeying to stand once again before the Chief Bard.

"A Fflam is thankful," he began, "and not one to look a gift horse—in this case, harp—in the mouth. But the strings were weak and worn. As for my wanderings, I was dined and feasted, welcomed and treated royally wherever I went. But the strings—there, you see, they're at it again!" he exclaimed, as several broke in two even as he spoke.

"I've only to take a breath!" Fflewddur lamented. "Why, the wretched things break at every word—" He stopped short and stared at the harp. "It would almost seem—" he murmured, his face turning sickly green. "But it can't be! But it is!" He groaned, looking all the more woebegone.

The Chief Bard was watching him closely and Fflewddur glanced sheepishly at him.

"Ah—the truth of it is," Fflewddur muttered, "I nearly froze to death in the wind, nearly drowned in the river, and my royal welcome was a royal cudgeling.

"Those beastly strings," he sighed. "Yes, they do break whenever I, ah, shall we say, adjust the facts. But facts are so gray and dreary, I can't help adding a little color. Poor things, they need it so badly."

"I have heard more of your wanderings than you might think," said the Chief Bard. "Have you indeed spoken all the truth? What of the old man you warmed with your cloak? The child you saved from the river? The lord at whose side you fought?"

Fflewddur blinked in astonishment. "Ah—yes, well, the truth of it is: it never occurred to me to mention them. They were much too dull and drab for any presentable tale at all."

"Yet those deeds were far more worthy than all your gallant fancies," said the Chief Bard, "for a good truth is purest gold that needs no gilding. You have the modest heart of the truly brave; but your tongue, alas, gallops faster than your head can rein it."

"No longer!" Fflewddur declared. "Never again will I stretch the truth!"

The harp strings tightened as if ready to break all at once.

"That is to say," Fflewddur added hastily, "never beyond what it can bear. A Fflam has learned his lesson. Forever!"

At this, a string snapped loudly. But it was only a small one.

Such is the tale of Fflewddur Fflam, the breaking of the strings, and the harp he carried in all his wanderings from that day forward.

And such is the end of it.

# Prydain Pronunciation Guide

**Achren** *AHK-ren*
**Adaon** *ah-DAY-on*
**Aeddan** *EE-dan*
**Angharad** *an-GAR-ad*
**Annuvin** *ah-NOO-vin*
**Arawn** *ah-RAWN*
**Arianllyn** *ahree-AHN-lin*

**Briavael** *bree-AH-vel*
**Brynach** *BRIHN-ak*

**Caer Cadarn** *kare KAH-darn*
**Caer Colur** *kare KOH-loor*
**Caer Dathyl** *kare DA-thil*
**Coll** *kahl*

**Dallben** *DAHL-ben*
**Doli** *DOH-lee*
**Don** *dahn*
**Dwyvach** *DWIH-vak*
**Dyrnwyn** *DUHRN-win*

**Edyrnion** *eh-DIR-nyon*
**Eiddileg** *eye-DILL-eg*
**Eilonwy** *eye-LAHN-wee*
**Ellidyr** *ELLI-deer*

**Fflewddur Fflam** *FLEW-der flam*

**Geraint** *GHER-aint*
**Goewin** *GOH-win*
**Govannion** *go-VAH-nyon*
**Gurgi** *GHER-ghee*
**Gwydion** *GWIH-dyon*
**Gwythaint** *GWIH-thaint*

**Islimach** *iss-LIM-ahk*

**Llawgadarn** *law-GAD-arn*
**Lluagor** *lew-AH-gore*
**Llunet** *LOO-net*
**Llyan** *lee-AHN*
**Llyr** *leer*

**Melyngar** *MELLIN-gar*
**Melynlas** *MELLIN-lass*

**Oeth-Anoeth** *eth-*AHN*-eth*

**Orddu** OR*-doo*

**Orgoch** OR*-gahk*

**Orwen** OR*-wen*

**Prydain** *prih-*DANE

**Pryderi** *prih-*DAY*-ree*

**Rhuddlum** ROOD*-lum*

**Rhun** *roon*

**Smoit** *smoyt*

**Taliesin** *tally-*ESS*-in*

**Taran** TAH*-ran*

**Teleria** *tell-*EHR*-ya*

## About the Author

Lloyd Alexander was born and raised in Philadelphia. As a boy he decided that he wanted to be a writer. "If reading offered any preparation for writing, there were grounds for hope. I had been reading as long as I could remember. Shakespeare, Dickens, Mark Twain, and so many others were my dearest friends and greatest teachers. I loved all the world's mythologies; King Arthur was one of my heroes; I played with a trash-can lid for a knightly shield, and my uncle's cane for the sword Excalibur."

During World War II, Mr. Alexander trained as a member of an army combat intelligence team in Wales. This ancient, rough-hewn country with its castles, mountains, and its own beautiful language made a tremendous impression on him, but not until years later did he realize that he had been given a glimpse of another enchanted kingdom.

After the war, while attending the University of Paris, he met his future wife, Janine. They were married, and moved back to Philadelphia, where Mr. Alexander wrote novel after novel. It was seven years before his first novel at last was published. Ten years later, he tried writing for children. It was, Mr. Alexander says, "the most creative and liberating experience of my life. In books for young people, I was able to express my own deepest feelings far more than I could ever do in writing for adults."

While doing historical research for a Welsh episode in his first children's book, *Time Cat*, he discovered such riches that he decided to save them for a whole book. He delved into all sorts of volumes, from anthropology to the writings of an eighteenth-century Welsh clergyman to the *Mabinogion*, the classic collection of Welsh legends. From his readings emerged such characters as Gwydion Son of Don, Arawn Death-Lord of Annuvin, Dallben the old enchanter, and the oracular pig Hen Wen. The landscape and mood of Prydain came from Mr. Alexander's vivid recollections of the land of Wales that had so enchanted him twenty years earlier.

The five books in the Chronicles of Prydain are *The Book of Three* (an ALA Notable Book), *The Black Cauldron* (a Newbery Honor Book), *The Castle of Llyr* (an ALA Notable Book), *Taran Wanderer*, and *The High King* (winner of the 1969 Newbery Medal). He followed the chronicles in 1973 with a collection of short stories, *The Foundling and Other Tales of Prydain*.